Sun-hee's Adventures Under the Land of Morning Calm

Sewelliana available from Evertype

La geste d'Aalis el Païs de Merveilles,
Old French verse by May Plouzeau, illustrated by Byron W. Sewell, 2016

The Aventures of Alys in Wondyr Lond,
Middle English verse by Brian S. Lee, illustrated by Byron W. Sewell, 2013

Alice's Adventures in an Appalachian Wonderland,
written by Byron W. Sewell & Victoria J. Sewell, illustrated by Byron W. Sewell, 2012

Sun-hee's Adventures Under the Land of Morning Calm,
written and illustrated by Victoria J. Sewell & Byron W. Sewell, 2016

선희의 조용한 아침의 나라 모험기 (*Seonhuiui Joyonghan Achim-ui Nala Moheomgi*),
Sun-hee in Korean, translated by Miyeong Kang, 2016

The Annotated Alice in Nurseryland, written and illustrated by Byron W. Sewell, 2016

Alice's Bad Hair Day in Wonderland: A Tangled Tale,
written and illustrated by Byron W. Sewell, 2013

Alix's Adventures in Wonderland: Lewis Carroll's Nightmare,
written and illustrated by Byron W. Sewell, 2011

Áloþk's Adventures in Goatland,
written by Byron W. Sewell, illustrated by Mahendra Singh, 2011

The Carrollian Tales of Inspector Spectre, written by Byron W. Sewell
with August A. Imholtz, Jr., illustrated by Byron W. Sewell, 2011

Snarks

The Haunting of the Snarkasbord, by Alison Tannenbaum,
Byron W. Sewell, Charlie Lovett, & August A. Imholtz, Jr, 2012

Snarkmaster: A Destiny in Eight Fits, written and illustrated by Byron W. Sewell, 2012

In the Boojum Forest, written and illustrated by Byron W. Sewell, 2014

Murder by Boojum: A Mystery in Eight Fits,
written and illustrated by Byron W. Sewell, 2014

Close Encounters of the Snarkian Kind, written and illustrated by Byron W. Sewell, 2016

Sun-hee's Adventures Under the Land of Morning Calm

A Korean tale inspired by Lewis Carroll's *Alice's Adventures in Wonderland*

by Victoria J. Sewell
and Byron W. Sewell

ILLUSTRATIONS BY
THE AUTHORS

2016

Published by Evertype, 73 Woodgrove, Portlaoise, R32 ENP6, Ireland.
www.evertype.com.

First published as *An, Sun-hee's Adventures Under the Land of Morning Calm*. Seoul: Sharing-Place, 1990, and in Korean translation as 선희의 조용한 아침의 나라 모험기 (*Seonhuiui Joyonghan Achim-ui Nala Moheomgi*). Seoul: Nanumjali (나눔자리), 1990.

Editor: Michael Everson.

A catalogue record for this book is available from the British Library.

ISBN-10 1-78201-172-2
ISBN-13 978-1-78201-172-9

Typeset in De Vinne Text, Mona Lisa, ENGRAVERS' ROMAN, *Liberty*, Hangyeole Gyeolche, and Songti TC by Michael Everson.

Cover: Michael Everson.

Printed by LightningSource.

Foreword

The prospect of publishing another of Byron and Victoria Sewell's works inspired by *Alice's Adventures in Wonderland* is a great pleasure. *An Sun-hee's Adventures Under the Land of Morning Calm* was published in English and in Korean translation in 1990; it has long been out of print and is nearly impossible to find anywhere. I am delighted to bring out this new edition, for English-speaking and Korean-speaking readers alike.

Hangul is an alphabetic script which organizes the letters into syllables, so instead of ㅎㅏㄴ, *han* is written 한 $^{ha}_{n}$. The McCune-Reischauer transliteration (MR) devised in 1937 was widely used and a variant of it is still used in North Korea. In 1995 a new system was developed, published in 2000 and called in English the Revised Romanization of Korean (RR). In Korean it is called 국어의 로마자 표기법 (written *Kugŏŭi Romaja P'yogipŏp* in MR and *Gugeoui Romaja Pyogibeop* in RR), 'Roman letter notation of the national language'. Though there are a number of fine transliteration and transcription details between them, the two systems differ chiefly in their treatment of some of the consonants (ㄱ ^{MR}*k*, ^{RR}*g*; ㅋ ^{MR}*k'*, ^{RR}*k*; ㄷ ^{MR}*t*, ^{RR}*d*; ㅌ ^{MR}*t'*, ^{RR}*t*; ㅂ ^{MR}*p*, ^{RR}*b*; ㅍ ^{MR}*p'*, ^{RR}*p*;

ㅈ [MR]*ch*, [RR]*j*; ㅉ [MR]*tch*, [RR]*jj*; ㅊ [MR]*ch'*, [RR]*ch*) and some of the vowels (ㅓ [MR]*ŏ*, [RR]*eo*; ㅕ [MR]*yŏ*, [RR]*yeo*; ㅝ [MR]*wŏ*, [RR]*wo*; ㅡ [MR]*ŭ*, [RR]*eu*; ㅢ [MR]*ŭi*, [RR]*ui*).

The RR system is promulgated in Korea, though most Koreans seem to prefer to use the older system in romanizations of their names, as in passports and the like. A practical romanization of this sort is found in our heroine's name: 안선희 *An Sun-hee* would be [MR]*An Sŏn-hŭi* or [RR]*An Seon-hui*, but the traditional form has been retained here. Other names have been revised to the modern RR standard, though footnotes give the Hangul text and MR reading where necessary.

Michael Everson
Portlaoise 2016

On Illustrating *Sun-hee*

There are many cultural references in the illustrations found in this book. It is probable that most Koreans would instantly recognize most of them, but since others might not, I offer here some discussion of the chief elements of interest. In these notes, references to "Korea" refer to The Republic of Korea.

p. 8: This opening scene depicts Sun-hee visiting a cemetery, where she has come to honour her ancestors. She observes the White Rabbit, costumed as a shaman, who is wearing a white robe. In Korea, the traditional colour for funerals and mourning is white (not black as in western cultures); white is a symbol associated with death. Those attending a funeral procession in rural Korea will usually be dressed in white. A magpie, a common bird in Korea, is perched on a branch of an ancient pine tree, which is one of many oriental symbols for long life. The White Rabbit is checking the time with an ancient Korean design of a sundial. The statue behind the White Rabbit is guarding the grave of an important person. These grass-covered hemispherical graves are quite commonly seen in Korean cemeteries.

p. 10: Sun-hee is dressed in a traditional ethnic costume. The dress's repetitive border design depicts two cranes, the crane being a symbol for long life. Objects on the sides of the rabbit hole shaft include a framed ancient map of Korea, traditional Korea ceramics, a pot (with 김치, [RR]*gimchi*, [MR]*kimch'i* written on it), a glass jar with a very old ginseng root in the lucky and valuable shape of a man, and a traditional Korean drum.

p. 12: Sun-hee is walking down a narrow paved pathway that is lined with ancient houses, featuring sliding decorative wooden framed doors that are covered in paper, similar to Japanese designs. The doors are all locked with traditional antique-style locks. The long "benches" are actually wooden steps into the first room. These have a physical and psychological purpose: the motion of stepping up to a different level, allows one to be aware that they are entering someone's private space. Hanging in front of each house is a lantern, indicating that everyone has gone to a temple or shrine to celebrate the Buddha's birthday. Hanging from each lamp is a short paper tag upon which the owner has written his name, hoping for good luck and a blessing. The pots on the step are *kimchi* pots.

p. 14: Sun-hee has shrunk and is dwarfed by the *kimchi* pot and step. The object on the antique Korean-style chest is the style of key that unlocks the locks on the sliding doors.

p. 18: Giant Sun-hee is crying huge tears that flood the passageway where she is trapped. The water is disturbed and comically alludes to the iconic waves depicted in Japanese woodblock prints, such as those in Katsushika Hokusai's *The Great Wave Off Kanagawa*.

p. 20: The Rat has been caught up in the stormy waves in the passageway and their menacing white caps appear to be trying to drown it.

p. 31: Sun-hee is about to enter the White Rabbit's house. The scroll on the wall says 兎舍 'rabbit house' in Chinese characters (the reading in Korean is 토사 *tosa*, and in Chinese *tù shè*; 兎 is a variant form of the more usual 兔. The object on the floor beneath it is a ceramic head rest (in lieu of a soft Western-style pillow). The slippers are suitable for the White Rabbit's feet, though a Korean would never have placed them inside, preferring to leave them outside on the step. The floor is covered in lacquered heavy paper in the traditional Korean-style underfloor heating *ondol*[1] that is used to keep the floor warm during cold weather.

p. 33: Giant Sun-hee is seen peering out of the White Rabbit's house. The structure on the right-hand side is the chimney, which was intentionally built away from the main house as a precaution against fire that might burn down the house which uses *ondol* heating. A small dragon named Nam-chul, is seen departing through the chimney. The house's beautiful roof is a traditional Korean design using ceramic half-cylindrical tiles.

p. 38: Sun-hee encounters a silkworm, sitting on an embroidery frame, busily working with silk thread on stretched silk fabric. The leaves in the background are mulberry leaves, the food eaten by silkworms. The Silkworm is smoking an opium pipe, and is wearing slippers to keep the silk fabric clean.

p. 45: Sun-hee's coiled neck extends up through the mulberry trees. She is confronted by a furious Magpie defending her nest. The contortions of Sun-hee's neck echo the *eum* and *yang* design in the centre of the Republic of Korea's national flag, known as *Taegeukgi*.

pp. 49 and 51: In these illustrations the Frog-Footman and Fish-Footman have been replaced by a Squid-Soldier and an Octopus-Soldier. This change was a response to the fact that Koreans did not wear wigs similar to those in western

1 An *ondol* (온돌), also called *gudeul* (구들[MR], *kudŭl*), in Korean traditional architecture, is underfloor heating that uses direct heat transfer from wood smoke to the underside of a thick masonry floor.

cultures. The Octopus-Soldier hands an invitation scroll to the Squid-Soldier. The vase in the lower right-hand corner is a floral arrangement in the Korean style, which is less tied to form and structures than the Japanese counterpart (*ikebana*). Korean floral design depends more on local flowers and plants and is elegant in its simplicity. As drawn here, the flowers mimic the style used on the faces of Korean playing cards.

p. 53: This is a scene inside Concubine Ok-paem's kitchen. Her hair style is based on a famous historical one worn by a member of the Royal court. The Temple Tiger, a spirit being said to guard Korean temples, is depicted in the primitive style used in some Korean folk art. At one time, centuries ago, tigers were common in the Korean peninsula, but none are now known to live there. The cook is carrying a pan full of very spicy peppers. Some pepper varieties in Korea are blistering hot. The "wavy" lines near the ceiling are a traditional oriental way to depict clouds and smoke.

p. 57: Sun-hee holds the pig-baby. In this Korean version he has been dressed appropriate for the Buddha's birthday celebrations. The houses in the background are based on the houses used long ago that had thatched roofs. Bundles of dried corn can be seen hanging from the eves.

p. 59: As Sun-hee is swinging in a forest she again encounters the Temple Tiger on a branch in the blossoming tree (either cherry or plum) and a Mountain Spirit. The blossoms and the iris are based on Korean playing card designs.

p. 62: Here the Temple Tiger slowly vanishes amidst the tree's falling blossoms.

p. 69: Here the Masked Hare—depicted as an actor with a Korean-style carved wooden mask representing a rabbit—and the Scholar—depicted with a ridiculously large Korean-style hat—are stuffing the Ginseng into a pot. They are standing atop a typical Korean-style wooden platform common to outdoor restaurants. The covered sheds seen in the background are used to shade growing ginseng on a farming or commercial basis, though traditionally ginseng was harvested in forests. Ginseng typically requires a minimum of seven years to mature and even then its potency is weak. Natural ginseng that has matured for perhaps 100 years has very great monetary value, depending upon the potency and the shape of the root.

p. 72: Tiny fairy-gardeners, wearing Korean playing card designs, are painting white *mugunghwa* blossoms pink. The *mugunghwa* (*Hibiscus syriacus*) is a common oriental deciduous shrub, known in Britain and Ireland as the rose mallow and in North America as the rose of Sharon. It is the Republic of Korea's national flower.

p. 75: In this royal procession, the King and Queen are wearing the Korean equivalent of crowns. They ride in a carriage pulled by famous decorative Korean-style horses. The guards following along are dressed in face-card cloaks.

p. 77: The King and Queen are playing *yut*, a game in which sticks are thrown. In this case they are playing with stiff snakes. The design at the lower left-hand corner is the game board. Stones are used for markers. In the background is a famous Korean gate design, with an ancient pine tree seen through the open doors. In the foreground, a few bamboo shoots are seen sprouting up.

p. 79: Sun-hee tries her luck at tossing the *yut* sticks, but her snakes refuse to be stiff and form a tangled mess instead. Behind the stone sculptures can be seen mature bamboo stalks and in the foreground more bamboo shoots are emerging.

p. 89: The Mock Turtleboat is depicted as an animated historical turtle ship (*geobukseon*), a large warship used by the Royal Korean Navy during the Joseon dynasty (15th-19th centuries), to engage invading naval ships. The most famous such event was the defeat of the Japanese fleet commanded by the formidable Toyotomi Hideyoshi, in the early 15th century. The Mock Turtleboat's companion is a mythical Phoenix bird, famous for emerging from the fire, something very symbolic and poignant with regard to Korea, which has suffered numerous disastrous invasions. Many temples in modern day Korea have been rebuilt several times after their destruction from invasions and wars.

p. 94: Here the Phoenix and Sun-hee are seen rushing to one of the famous Royal palaces in Seoul, where the trial is about to begin.

p. 97: In the throne room the White Rabbit, as court musician, plays a large bamboo flute (called a *daegeum*). The King sits upon a traditional throne with decorative deer incorporated into the armrests of the design. Behind the throne are traditional sliding paper-covered doors.

p. 100: Sun-hee and the Ginseng are seated on the floor. The man in spectacles is a caricature of the last Crown Prince of Korea, who was installed by the Japanese in 1926 after their invasion. He was very unpopular with the Korean people because of his collaboration with the Japanese. The guard standing beside him wears yet another card-face cloak and holds an axe of ancient Korean design.

p. 105: Sun-hee has begun to grow again into a giant, reaching all the way into the ceiling of the elaborately decorated throne room. Some of the beams are carved as the heads of dragons. She has tipped over some of the other characters in the tale.

p. 107: Depicted here are all of the familiar characters of the East Asian zodiac who are in attendance at the trial: rat, ox, tiger, rabbit, dragon, snake, horse, sheep, monkey, cock (perhaps incorrectly drawn here as a chicken), dog, and pig. Most of these animals have made earlier appearances in the telling of this Korean adaptation of Carroll's famous tale.

All of the illustrations were a collaborative effort by both myself and my wife Victoria, and both of our initials appear on them all. While in Korea we had very limited access to drawing materials. All preliminary sketches were done in pencil on the sheets of rice paper that are normally used for Korean-style brush painting. I inked the final drawings using India ink on relatively transparent vellum, which before electronic drafting was still in use for technical drafting. All of the drawings were inked with the tiniest brushes that we could purchase in their rather remote location near Yeochun, close to the southern tip of the Korean peninsula. Some of the brushes probably had fewer than ten hairs. The final image sizes were approximately 6.25 × 9.75 inches. Using these small brushes was tedious and in the middle of this effort my vision suddenly (in mid-brush stroke) changed to double-vision, forcing me to make a special trip to Seoul to get eyeglasses. Two of the illustrations were initially drawn by Victoria, these being the illustrations on pages 33 and 72. The former has been coloured by Michael Everson for the front cover of this edition; the illustration on p. 45 was coloured by pencil by a Korean artist (whose name has, alas, been lost) for the first edition, and appears on the back cover.

Byron W. Sewell
with Victoria J. Sewell
Hurricane, West Virginia, 2016

Sun-hee's Adventures Under the Land of Morning Calm

To
Yu-jin (유 진),
Kwon Hyon-chai (권 현채),
and to
Sandor and Beth Burstein,
the best of two worlds.

Contents

When gingko leaves were falling like drops of sun,
  Sleeping, I clung to the footsteps of a frightened hare.
Now the wind scatters the morning calm of long ago—
  Ah! Do you hear the court musician's song?
A thousand Li apart, below
  only in dreams we *kŭmun'go*.[2]

—Victoria J. Sewell
1985

2 *geomungo*—(거문고, [MR]*kŏmun'go*, pronounced "come and go")—a six string instrument similar to a zither, which originated in the 7th century, played with a pick held in the right hand, This poem parodies a 16th-century poem by Yi Mae-chang (이매창), "When pear blossoms..."

Chapter I

Down the Tumulus

Sun-hee[3] was beginning to get very tired of watching her sister swing back and forth on the long rope hanging from the gingko tree she was sitting under. Sun-hee felt drowsy from eating so many rice cakes on this bright *Chuseok* Day.[4] As her eyes drooped lower she imagined her sister looked like a multi-coloured kite caught on a tree branch, helplessly fluttering on the breeze, her long pigtail flapping like the lost end of a kite string.

She was twisting the iris root that was tied in her hair, staring at the words "long life" carved into the root and wondering if she could stand a long life as bored as she was at this moment, when suddenly a White Rabbit in a white *jeogori*[5] ran close by her.

---

3 Sun-hee (선희 (仙姬), [RR]*Seon-hui*, [MR]*Sŏn-hŭi*)—literally, "fairyland girl".

4 *Chuseok* Day (추석 [MR]*Ch'usŏk*)—a major national holiday, celebrated on the 15th day of the 8th lunar month, roughly equivalent to Thanksgiving Day in America, occurring on the first full moon of the harvest season. One primary activity is to dress in traditional costume and visit the tombs of one's ancestors.

5 *jeogori* (저고리, [MR]*chŏgori*)—the traditional man's blouse or shirt.

There was nothing so very remarkable in that; nor did Sun-hee think it so very much out of the way to hear the Rabbit say to itself, "Oh dear! Oh dear! I shall be too late!" but when the Rabbit *actually took a sun clock from out of its jeogori,* and looked at it, and then hurried on, Sun-hee started to her feet, for it flashed across her mind that she had never before seen a rabbit in a mourning *jeogori,* or a sun clock that wasn't imbedded in stone, much less in someone's pocket, and burning with curiosity, she ran across the field after it. She was just in time to see it pop down a large rabbit-hole in the side of a *tumulus.*[6] "That explains why he's dressed in white," Sun-hee said to herself; "he's been to someone's funeral!"

In another moment down went Sun-hee after it, never once considering how in the world she was to get out again.

The rabbit-hole went straight on like a cave for some way, then dipped suddenly down, so suddenly that Sun-hee had not a moment to think about stopping herself before she found herself falling down what seemed to be a deep well.

Either the well was very deep, or she fell very slowly, for she had plenty of time as she went down to look about her and to wonder what was going to happen next. First, she tried to look down and make out what she was coming to, but it was too dark to see anything; then she looked at the sides of the well and noticed that they were filled with chests and bookshelves; here and there she saw framed calligraphy and maps at important places along the walls. She took down a clay pot from one of the shelves as she passed: it was labeled "KIMCHI"[7] but to her great disappointment it was empty. She did not want to drop the pot, for fear of breaking it and

6 *tumulus*—the traditional burial mound, shaped in a nearly perfect hemisphere, almost always covered in grass. Ancient tumuli often contain the belongings of the deceased for his or her use in the afterlife.

7 *kimchi* (김치, [RR]*gimchi*, [MR]*kimch'i*)—the most famous and unique Korean dish, consisting of fermented cabbage, garlic, hot red pepper, radish, and usually fish, prepared in a salt brine and traditionally stored in pots undergound during the winter.

김치

damaging someone's *gibun*[8] for the day, so managed to put it into a wedding chest as she fell past it.

Down, down, down. Would the fall *never* come to an end? "I wonder if I shall fall right through the earth!" she said aloud. "How funny it'll seem to come out among the people that drink *maté* and throw *bolas*! The Patagonians, I think—" (she was rather glad there was no one listening, this time, as she wasn't sure if she had used the right word) "—but I shall have to ask them what the name of the country is, you know. "Please, *Señora,* is this Argentina?" And she tried to bow deeply as she spoke—fancy, bowing as you're falling through the air!

Thump! thump! down she came upon a heap of bamboo and dry leaves, and the fall was over.

Sun-hee was not a bit hurt, and she jumped up on to her feet in a moment: she looked up, but it was all dark overhead: before her was another long passage, and the White Rabbit was still in sight, hurrying down it. There was not a moment to be lost; away went Sun-hee like the wind, and was just in time to hear it say, as it turned a corner, "Oh my ears and whiskers, how late it's getting!" She was close behind it when she turned the corner, but the Rabbit was no longer to be seen; she found herself in a long, narrow alley, which was lit up by lanterns hanging from the eaves. "These must be left from Buddha's Birthday,"[9] she thought to herself.

There were doors all along the alley, and Sun-hee went all the way up one side and down the other until she came to high stone walls blocking the exits. As she tried every door she thought to herself, "It must still be *Chuseok* Day as all the

8 *gibun* (기분, [MR]*kibun*)—the state of one's inner feelings, self-esteem, prestige, morale, and "face." There is no English equivalent, but may be roughly approximated by 'mood'.

9 Buddha's Birthday—another great national holiday, celebrated on the 8th day of the 4th lunar month, characterized by the lighting of lanterns to celebrate the birthday of the Buddha.

海井

shops are closed." She walked sadly down the middle of the alley, wondering how she was ever to get out again.

Suddenly she came upon a low scholar's desk, all made of paulownia wood; there was nothing on it but a tiny brass key, and Sun-hee's first idea was that this might belong to one of the locks on the doors in the alley; but *aigo!*[10] either the locks were too large, or the key too small, and it would not open any of them. However, on the second time around, she came upon a low screen she had not noticed before, and behind it was a little door; she tried the little brass key in the lock, and to her great delight it fitted!

Sun-hee opened the door and found that it led into a small passage, about the size for a bat to go through; she knelt down and looked along the passage into the loveliest secret garden she'd ever seen. How she longed to get out of that dark alley, and wander about among the bright orchids and those cool reflecting ponds. She thought of all the times she played on the seesaw hoping to catch a glimpse beyond the secret garden wall into the alley on the other side. Now she was in the alley wanting back in the garden; how curious she thought it was when an old *harabeoji*[11] had caught her peering over the garden wall and referred to her as 'A thirsty cow looking into a dry well'—it did seem rather dusty and dry in this alley—how sad that, at the time, she didn't think of asking him in for a drink. She found she couldn't get her head through the doorway; "and even if my head would go through," thought poor Sun-hee, "it would be of very little use without my shoulders. Oh, how I wish I could fold up like a fan! I think I could if only I knew how to begin."

There seemed to be no use in waiting by the little door, so she went back to the desk, half hoping she might find another key on it, or at any rate a scroll of rules for folding people up

10 *aigo!* (아이고)—a very common exclamatory word.

11 *harabeoji* (할아버지, MR*haraboji*)—the familar form of the term used to address one's own grandfather, but often applied to grandfathers in general.

like fans: this time she found a little bottle on it ("which certainly was not here before," said Sun-hee), and tied around the neck of the bottle was a rice paper label, with the words "DRINK ME" beautifully printed on it in large Hangul characters.[12] Sun-hee ventured to taste it, and, finding it very nice (it had, in fact, a sort of mixed flavour of sesame, pinenut, dried octopus, and garlic), she very soon finished it off.

"What a curious feeling!" said Sun-hee, "I must be folding up like a fan!" And so it was indeed: she was now approximately the size of a bat; just the right size to go through the little door into that lovely secret garden. But, alas for poor Sun-hee! for when she got to the door, she found she had forgotten the little brass key, and when she went back to the scholar's desk for it, she found she could not possibly reach it. She could see the tassel that was tied to the end of the key hanging over the edge of the desk, but it was too high; and although she was the size of a bat, she, alas, lacked its wings to fly up and get it, and being very frustrated sat down and cried.

Soon her eye fell on a little lacquered box that was lying under the desk; she opened it, and found in it a very small rice cake in the shape of a crescent moon, on which the words "EAT ME" were beautifully marked in raisins. "Well, I'll eat

12 *hangul* (한글, [RR]*han-guel*, [MR]*han'gŭl*)—the phonetic alphabet developed during the reign of the great Yi Dynasty ruler King Sejong (1418-1450), and one of Korea's great literary achievements. This alphabet has largely replaced the use of Chinese characters in written Korean, and has greatly facilitated Korean literacy.

it," said Sun-hee. So she set to work, and very soon finished off the cake.

Chapter II

The Pool of Tears

"Curiouser and curiouser!" cried Sun-hee (she was so much surprised that for the moment she quite forgot how to speak Korean properly). "Now I'm rolling out like the largest scroll that ever was! Good-bye feet!" (for when she looked down at her feet, they seemed to be almost out of sight, they were getting so far off).

Just at this moment her head struck against the eave of a shop; in fact, she was now higher than the *Emile* Bell.[13] and she at once took up the little golden key and hurried off to the garden door.

Poor Sun-hee! It was as much as she could do, lying down on one side, to look through into the secret garden with one eye; but to get through was more hopeless than "pushing an ox through a mouse-hole"! She knelt down and began to cry again. She went on shedding buckets of tears until there was a large pool around her and reaching halfway down the alley.

13 *Emile* Bell—the most famous existing Silla Dynasty Korean bronze bell, weighing nearly 20 tons and approximately eleven feet high, The bell, when struck, makes a mournful peal, like the sound of a child calling for its mother, "Emi… lie."

After a time she heard a little pattering of feet in the distance, and she hastily dried her eyes to see what was coming. It was the White Rabbit returning, splendidly dressed in a flowing *durumagi*,[14] with a chop in one hand and a large fan in the other; he came trotting along in a great hurry, muttering to himself, as he came, "Oh! Concubine Ok-baem![15] Oh! Ok-baem! Oh! Wo'n't she be savage if I've kept her waiting!"

Sun-hee began in a low, timid voice, "If you please, Sir—" The Rabbit started violently, dropped the chop and the fan, and scurried away into the darkness as hard as he could go.

Sun-hee took up the fan and the chop, and, as the alley was very hot, she kept fanning herself all the while she went on talking. "Dear, dear! How queer everything is today! And yesterday things went on just as usual. I wonder if I've changed in the night? I'll try to say '*How doth the mythical—*'," and she cupped her hand to her ear as she did when listening through the screen to the scholar giving lessons to the little boys, and began to repeat it, but her voice sounded hoarse and strange, and the words did not come the same as she had heard:—

"How doth the mythical HAETAE[16]
Defend wooden temples,
And cast the fire gods from his way;
Eating fire is simple!

"How cheerfully he seems to grin,
How neatly spreads his claws,
And welcomes little embers in
With gently smiling jaws!"

14 *durumagi* (두루마기, [MR]*turumagi*)—a topcoat, usually worn by old men, and usually white or light blue.

15 *Ok-baem*— (옥뱀, [MR]*Ok-paem*)—literally, "Jade Serpent".

16 *haetae* (해태, [MR]*haet'ae*)—an imaginary beast, one of whose functions is to guard structures such as temples from the hazards of fire, which it has the ability to eat.

海井

"I'm sure those are not the right words," said poor Sun-hee, and her eyes filled with tears again as she went on, "I must have changed after all. Who am I then?"

As she said this she looked down at her hands, and was surprised to find the Rabbit's chop in her left hand had grown suddenly heavier, and so large her tiny hand would no longer fit around it, so she dropped it. "How is that possible?" she thought, "I must be growing small again." She got up and went over to a *kimchi* pot sitting beside a door to measure herself by it, and found she could now barely see over the lid of the pot, and was going on shrinking rapidly. She soon found out that the cause of this was the fan she was holding, and she dropped it hastily, just in time to save herself from shrinking away altogether.

"That was a narrow escape!" said Sun-hee, a good deal frightened at the sudden change, but very glad to find herself still in existence. "And now for the secret garden!" And she ran with all speed back to the little door; but, *aigo!* the little door was shut again, and the little brass key was lying on the scholar's desk as before, "and things are worse than ever," thought the poor child, "for I never was so small as this before, never!"

As she said these words her foot slipped, and in another moment, splash! she was up to her chin in salt-water. Her first idea was that she had somehow fallen into the Yellow Sea. However, she soon made out that she was in the pool of tears which she had wept when she was as tall as the *Emile* Bell.

"I wish I hadn't cried so much!" said Sun-hee, as she swam about trying to find her way out. "I shall be punished for it now, I suppose, by being drowned in my own tears!"

Just then something dark and very large pushed by her on an enormous wave that arose from the water like a clawing hand; at first she thought it must be a whale or giant octopus, but she remembered how small she was now and that this really wasn't the sea, and she soon made out it was only a mouse, that had slipped in like herself.

"O Mouse, do you know the way out of this pool?" said Sun-hee, assuming the mouse could talk, "I am very tired of swimming about here, O Mouse!" The Mouse looked at her rather inquisitively, and seemed to her to wink with one of its little eyes, but it said nothing.

"Perhaps it doesn't understand Korean," thought Sun-hee. "I daresay it's a Japanese mouse, come over with Hideyoshi." So she began: *"Konban wa!"* which were the first two words in her Japanese lesson-book. The Mouse gave a sudden leap out of the water, and seemed to quiver all over with fright. "Oh, I am sorry!" cried Sun-hee hastily, "I am quite surprised you are frightened upon hearing Japanese."

"Not be afraid of Japanese!" cried the Mouse in a shrill, passionate voice. "Wouldn't you be afraid if you had seen Hideyoshi's armada from the hull of Admiral Yi's 'turtleboat'!"[17]

"Well, perhaps," said Sun-hee in a soothing tone: "I wasn't aware you were there."

"I wasn't," cried the Mouse giving another sudden shudder, but one of my ancestors was, and I assure you his tale is quite chilling!"

"Must be hereditary," thought Sun-hee as she watched the Mouse's tail quiver.

"Follow me," said the Mouse. "I know the way to the shore." It was high time to go, for the pool was getting quite crowded with other birds and animals that had fallen into it: there was a Magpie, an Ibis, a Crane, a Woodpecker, and several other curious creatures. Sun-hee led the way, and the whole party swam to shore.

17 turtleboat—an armour plated boat used with devastating effect by Korea's great national hero Admiral Yi Sun-shin (1545-1598) to eventually break the back of the Japanese invasion of Korea in 1592, led by the powerful Japanese general, Hideyoshi.

Chapter III

A Game of *Tuho*[18] and a Long Tale

They were indeed a queer-looking party that assembled on the bank—the birds with draggled feathers, the animals with their fur clinging close to them, and all dripping wet, cross, and uncomfortable.

The first question of course was, how to get dry again: they had a consultation about this, and after a few minutes it seemed quite natural to Sun-hee to find herself talking familiarly with them, as if she had known them all her life. Indeed, she had quite a long argument with the Crane, who at last turned sulky, and would only say, "I'm older than you, and must know better." And this Sun-hee would not allow without knowing how old it was, and, as the Crane positively refused to tell its age, there was no more to be said.

18 *Tuho* is a game originally popular among royal families and the upper class. The game is similar to horseshoes: *tuho* players attempt to throw arrows into the top of a narrow-necked wooden jar. The score is determined by the number of arrows in the jar. Today, *tuho* is played by people from all classes.

At last the Mouse, who seemed to be a person of some authority among them, called out, "Sit down, all of you, and listen to me! *I'll* soon make you dry enough!" They all sat down at once, in a large ring, with the Mouse in the middle. Sun-hee kept her eyes anxiously fixed on it, for she felt sure she would catch a bad cold if she did not get dry very soon.

"Ahem!" said the Mouse with an important air. "Are you all ready? This is the driest thing I know.[19] Silence all round, if you please! 'Because the language of our country is different from that of China, the spoken language of Korea is not suited to the Chinese characters. For this reason, even though there are many people in the uneducated population who want to communicate—'"

"Ugh!" said the Crane, with a shiver.

"I beg your pardon!" said the Mouse, frowning, but very politely. "Did you speak?"

"Not I!" said the Crane, hastily.

"I thought you did," said the Mouse. "I proceed. '—even though there are many people in the uneducated population who want to communicate, in the end they cannot express their concerns. Saddened by this—'"

"By *what*?" said the Magpie.

"By *this*," the Mouse replied rather crossly: "of course you know what 'this' means."

"I know what 'this' means well enough, when *I* find a thing," said the Magpie: "it's generally a frog, or a worm. The question is, what saddened King Sejong?"

The Mouse did not notice this question, but hurriedly went on, "'Saddened by this, I have had twenty-eight letters newly

19 The paragraph read by the Mouse is from the *Hunminjeongeum* (훈민정음, [MR]*Hunminjŏngŭm*, lit. 'The Proper Sounds for the Instruction of the People'), and explains King Sejong's motivation for devising the new alphabet. This is the text which introduced the hangul alphabet for the Korean language. It was announced in Volume 102 of the *Annals of King Sejong*, and its formal supposed publication date, the 9th of October 1446, a day now celebrated as Hangul Day in the Republic of Korea.

made. It is my wish that all the people may easily learn these letters and that they be convenient for daily use—' How are you getting on now, my dear?" it continued, turning to Sun-hee as it spoke.

"As wet as ever," said Sun-hee in a melancholy tone: "it doesn't seem to dry me at all."

"In that case," said the Ibis solemnly, rising to its feet, "I move that the meeting adjourn, for the immediate adoption of more energetic remedies—"

"Speak properly!" said the Eaglet. "I don't know the meaning of half those long words, and, what's more, I don't believe you do either!" And the Eaglet bent down its head to hide a smile: some of the other birds tittered audibly.

"What I was going to say," said the Ibis in an offended tone, "was, that the best thing to get us dry would be a game of *tuho*."

"How do you play *tuho*?" said Sun-hee; not that she much wanted to know, but the Ibis had paused as if it thought that *somebody* ought to speak, and no one else seemed inclined to say anything.

"Why," said the Ibis, "the best way to explain it is to do it." (And, as you might like to try the thing yourself, some day, I will tell you how the Ibis managed it.)

First it set out a narrow-necked wooden jar and handed out arrows to all the party. Then they began throwing the arrows toward the jar to see who could get the most in. They began to get so excited and forgot to take turns (which was against the rules, to tell the truth), and they began throwing when they liked, and left off when they liked, so that it was not easy to know which players had got their arrows in the jar and which ones had missed. However, when they had been playing half an hour or so, and were quite dry again, the Ibis suddenly called out, "The game is over!" and they all crowded round it, panting, and asking, "But who has won?"

This question the Ibis could not answer without a great deal of thought, and it stood for a long time with one finger pressed upon its forehead, while the rest waited in silence. At last the Ibis said, "*Everybody* has won, and *all* must have prizes."

"But who is to give the prizes?" quite a chorus of voices asked.

"Why, *she*, of course," said the Ibis, pointing to Sun-hee with one finger; and the whole party at once crowded round her, calling out, in a confused way, "Prizes! Prizes!"

Sun-hee had no idea what to do, and in despair she put her hand in her pocket, and pulled out a box of *suksilgwa*[20] (luckily the salt water had not got into it), and handed them round as prizes. There was exactly one a-piece, all round.

"But she must have a prize herself, you know," said the Mouse.

"Of course," the Ibis replied very gravely. "What else have you got in your pocket?" it went on, turning to Sun-hee.

"Only a thimble," said Sun-hee sadly.

"Hand it over here," said the Ibis.

Then they all crowded round her once more, while the Ibis solemnly presented the thimble, saying, "We beg your acceptance of this elegant thimble"; and, when it had finished this short speech, they all cheered.

Sun-hee thought the whole thing very absurd, but they all looked so grave that she did not dare to laugh; and, as she could not think of anything to say, she simply bowed, and took the thimble, looking as solemn as she could.

The next thing was to eat the *suksilgwa*: this caused some noise and confusion, as the large birds complained that they could not taste theirs, and the small ones choked and had to be patted on the back. However, it was over at last, and they sat down again in a ring, and begged the Mouse to tell them something more.

20 *Suksilgwa* is a variety of *hangwa*, Korean traditional confectionery, made by boiling various fruits, ginger or nuts in water and then re-formed into their original fruit-shape or other shapes.

After each finding a spot to dry out, the Mouse replied to Sun-hee, "While we are here, shall I tell you how I came to be in this sorrowful place with these feathered, fidgety creatures as my court?"

"If you don't mind—" began Sun-hee thinking she really should be on her way, and moved to get up.

"I don't mind at all!" exclaimed the Mouse, "and please do make yourself comfortable. Mine is a long and sad tale!" said the Mouse, turning to Sun-hee, and sighing.

"It is a long tail, certainly," said Sun-hee, looking down with wonder at the Mouse's tail; "but why do you call it sad?" And she kept on puzzling about it while the Mouse was speaking, so that her idea of the tale was something like this:—

"A *yangban*[21] said to
a mouse, Come
from some rival
house, 'I
too seek the
throne: *No*
King need
sit alone.—
Now, I'll
take no re-
tort: Let me
come join
your court;
When I help
rule this land
I'll come into
my own.' Said
the mouse to
this cur, 'Such
a country,
dear sir, With
two Kings
and two
Queens
would be
one royal
mess!'
'Save the
State,
call the
hangman,'
With
calm
said the
yangban:
'We'll
try
the
old
chiefs
and
con-
demn
them
to
death.'

21 *yangban* (양반)—an aristocrat.

"'As white as a magpie's breast!'" clacked the Crane to the Woodpecker, who had fallen asleep and dreamt the Crane's leg was a tree and had begun furiously pecking on it. "I truly was asleep!" screamed the Woodpecker.

"I beg your pardon," said Sun-hee very gently, hoping to calm the disturbance: "you had got to the third bend, I think?"

"I had not!" cried the Mouse sharply and very angrily.

"A knot!" said Sun-hee, always ready to make herself useful, and looking anxiously about her. "Oh, do let me help to undo it!"

"I shall do nothing of the sort," said the Mouse, tired of the interruptions. "You insult me by talking such nonsense!"

"I didn't mean it!" pleaded poor Sun-hee. "But you're so easily offended, you know!"

The Mouse only growled in reply, getting up and walking away.

"Please come back, and finish your story!" Sun-hee called after it. And the others all joined in chorus "Yes, please do!" But the Mouse only shook its head, and walked a little quicker.

"What a pity it wouldn't stay!" sighed the Woodpecker, as soon as it was quite out of sight. "Well, it is partially your fault it left," mumbled the Crane who was busily packing mud and leaves onto the cuts on his leg. "I'm the one who should be insulted and leave," said the Magpie staring at his breast of white feathers.

"I wonder if there are any dragons here," said Sun-hee aloud, addressing nobody in particular. "With all this water you'd expect to see one." Noticing she had gotten their attention, she continued: "It's said that a giant, golden carp from the deep ocean turned into a yellow dragon and rose into the sky on his chariot of clouds," Sun-hee said with much enthusiasm and wonder.

This speech caused a remarkable sensation among the Party. "'Feet, don't fail me!'" cried the Crane as he bowed and hurried off at once. One old Magpie began wrapping itself up very carefully, remarking, "I really must be getting home: the night-air doesn't suit my throat!" Sun-hee replied, "It is quite rude of all of you to hurry off before I finish my story: 'It's like eating chicken before removing the feathers'!" At this remark the Ibis mumbled, "'Smile and slap a bird in the beak—'" and hurried her children off to bed. Sun-hee was soon left alone.

"I wish I hadn't mentioned the golden carp!" she said to herself in a melancholy tone. Sun-hee began to cry again, for she felt very lonely and low-spirited. In a little while, however, she again heard a little pattering of footsteps in the distance and she looked up eagerly, half hoping that the Mouse had changed his mind and was coming back to finish his story.

CHAPTER IV

The Rabbit Sends in a Little Dragon

It was the White Rabbit, trotting slowly back again, and looking anxiously about as it went, as if it had lost something; and she heard it muttering to itself, "Concubine Ok-baem! Oh, Ok-baem! Oh my dear paws! Oh my fur and whiskers! She'll get me executed, as sure as weasels are weasels! Where can I have dropped them, I wonder?" Sun-hee guessed in a moment that it was looking for the fan and chop, and she very good-naturedly began hunting about for them, but they were nowhere to be seen.

Very soon the Rabbit noticed Sun-hee, as she went hunting about, and called out to her, in an angry tone, "Why, Sook-yung, what are you doing here? Run home this moment, and fetch me a chop and a fan! Quick, now!" And Sun-hee was so much frightened that she ran off at once in the direction it pointed to, without trying to explain the mistake that it had made.

"He took me for his housemaid," she said to herself as she ran. "How surprised he'll be when he finds out who I am! But I'd better take him his fan and chop—that is, if I can find them." As she said this, she came upon a neat little house, and through the sliding doors on one wall she saw a calligraphic scroll which read "Rabbit Hutch." Laying just inside there was a rather large pair of house slippers that looked very much like they would fit the White Rabbit, and a *yo*[22] was still lying flat on the floor as if someone had left in a hurry. She removed her shoes and hurried in, in great fear lest she should meet the real Sook-yung, and be turned out of the house before she had found the fan and chop.

Soon she found her way into a tidy little room with a chest against one wall, and on it (as she had hoped) a fan and several sizes of chops: she took up the fan and one of the chops, and was just going to leave the room, when her eye fell upon a little bottle that stood inside a comb box under the looking-glass. There was no label this time with the words "DRINK ME", but nevertheless she uncorked it and put it to her lips. "I know something interesting is sure to happen," she said to herself.

Before she had drunk half the bottle, she found her head pressing against the ceiling, and had to stoop to save her neck from being broken. She hastily put down the bottle, saying to herself, "That's quite enough—I hope I don't grow any more—As it is, I ca'n't slide the doors open—I do wish I hadn't drunk quite so much!"

It was too late to wish that! She went on growing, and growing, and very soon had to kneel down on the floor, her head in the rafters, one foot in the direction of the kitchen, and the other jammed against the tiny chest where the bottle had been.

Luckily for Sun-hee, the little magic bottle had now had its full effect, and she grew no larger: still it was very uncomfortable, and, as there seemed to be no sort of chance

22 *yo* (요)—the traditional bedding, a relatively thick pallet, placed on the floor, which can be rolled or folded up when not in use.

of her ever getting out of the room again, no wonder she felt unhappy.

"It was much pleasanter at home," thought poor Sun-hee, "when one wasn't always growing larger and smaller, and being ordered about by mice and rabbits. I almost wish I hadn't gone down that *tumulus*—and yet—it's rather curious, you know, this sort of life! I do wonder what can have happened to me! When I used to read fairy tales, I fancied that kind of thing never happened, and now here I am in the middle of one! There should be a book written about me. And when I grow up, I'll write one—but I'm grown up now," she added in a sorrowful tone: "At least there's no room to grow up any more *here*."

"Sook-yung! Sook-yung!" said the voice. "Fetch me my chop this moment!" Then came a little pattering of feet on the porch. Sun-hee knew it was the Rabbit coming to look for her, and she trembled till she shook the house, quite forgetting that she was now about a thousand times as large as the Rabbit, and had no reason to be afraid of it.

Presently the Rabbit came up to the door, and tried to slide it open; but as Sun-hee was wedged against it, that attempt proved a failure.

There was a long silence after this, and Sun-hee could hear whispers now and then; such as "However are we going to get her out?" "'Like pulling a turtle out of its shell!'" "We'll pull her out by her feet!" She spread out her hand and made a snatch at the air through an open window. There were two little shrieks, and the sound of splintering wood and tearing paper. She concluded that they (whoever "they" were) were trying to climb in the window and squeeze her out. "That wo'n't do!" thought Sun-hee, and wedged her knee against the window so they wouldn't try that again.

She waited for some time without hearing anything more: at last came a rumbling of little cart-wheels, and the sound of a good many voices all talking together: she made out the words: "Where's the ladder?—Why, I didn't bring but one. Nam-chul's got the other—Nam-chul! Fetch it here, boy!—Here, put 'em up at this corner by the chimney.—No, tie 'em together first. Here, Nam-chul! Catch hold of this rope—Will the roof bear?—Mind that loose end-tile—Oh, it's coming down! Move that screen!" (a loud crash)—"Now, who's to go down the chimney?—Nam-chul's got to go down—Dragons don't mind fire and smoke!—Here, Nam-chul! The Master says you've got to go down the chimney and come up through the hearth in the kitchen!"

"Oh, so Nam-chul's got to come down the chimney, has he?" said Sun-hee to herself. "Why, they seem to put everything upon Nam-chul! I wouldn't be in Nam-chul's place for a good deal; my foot is in the kitchen and the fireplace is narrow, to be sure; but I think I can kick a little!"

She pushed her sock off and placed her toes against the hearth (thankful that the White Rabbit hadn't time this day to stir the fire), and waited till she felt the soot and coals from the fireplace move: then, saying to herself "This is Nam-chul," she gave a sharp kick, and waited to see what would happen next.

The first thing she heard was a general chorus of "There goes Nam-chul!" then the Rabbit's voice alone—"'A dragon soars from the well'—Catch him, you by the wall!" then silence, and then another confusion of voices—"Hold up his head—Bring the *makgeolli*[23]—Don't choke him—What happened to you? Tell us all about it!"

Last came a little feeble, squeaking voice. ("That's Nam-chul," though Sun-hee.) "Well, I hardly know—No more, thank you; I'm better now—but I'm a deal too flustered to tell you—all I know is, something jumped up at me like 'a green frog on a watermelon vine' and up I go 'high enough to pluck stars like berries!'"

"So you were, old fellow!" said the others.

"We must burn the house down!" said the Rabbit's voice.

23 *makgeolli* (막걸리, [MR]*makkŏlli*)—an alcoholic drink brewed from rice and traditionally made at home or in rural areas.

And Sun-hee called out, as loud as she could, "'After many claps of thunder, the fire-sword will fall!'"

There was a dead silence instantly, and Sun-hee thought to herself "I wonder what they will do next! If they had any sense, they'd take the roof off." After a moment or two they began moving about again, and Sun-hee heard the Rabbit say "A barrowful will do, to begin with."

"A barrowful of *what?*" thought Sun-hee. But she had not long to doubt, for the next moment a shower of little pebbles came rattling in at the window, and some of them hit her in the face. "I'll put a stop to this," she said to herself, and shouted out "You'd better not do that again!" which produced another dead silence.

Sun-hee noticed, with some surprise, that the pebbles were all turning into gingko nuts as they lay on the floor, and a bright idea came into her head. "If I eat one of these nuts," she thought, "It's sure to make *some* change in my size, and, as it ca'n't possibly make me larger, it must make me smaller, I suppose."

So she swallowed one of the nuts, and was delighted to find that she began shrinking directly. As soon as she was small enough to get through the door, she ran out of the house, and found quite to crowd of little animals and birds waiting outside. The poor little dragon, Nam-chul, was in the middle, being held up by two small bears, who were giving it something out of a bottle. They all made a rush at Sun-hee the moment she appeared; but she ran off as hard as she could, and soon found herself in a thick grove of bamboo.

"The first thing I've got to do," said Sun-hee to herself, as she wandered about in the bamboo, "is to grow to my right size again; and the second thing is to find my way out into that lovely secret garden. I think that will be the best plan. Let me see—how is it to be managed? I suppose I ought to eat or drink something or other; but the great question is 'What?'"

The great question certainly was "What?" Sun-hee looked all around her at the flowers and blades of grass, but she could not see anything that looked like the right thing to eat or drink under the circumstances. There was a large tree growing near her, its leaves about the same size as herself; and, when she looked at it, it appeared to have *gaeng yeot*[24] strung across its leaves and limbs. It occurred to her that she might as well get a closer look to see if it was indeed something edible; and, seeing a table resting on a root, decided. to climb up and see if she could reach the candy.

She stretched herself up on tiptoe, and peeped over the edge of the table, and her eyes immediately met those of a large silkworm, that was sitting on top of an embroidery frame covered in blue silk. He was busily embroidering a design into the silk—pulling thread from one of his ends and sewing with the other—quietly smoking on a long opium pipe, and taking not the smallest notice of her or of anything else.

24 *gaeng yeot* (갱엿, [MR]*kaeng yŏt*))—a variety of Korean confectionary made from steamed rice, glutinous rice, glutinous sorghum, corn, sweet potatoes, or mixed grains. The steamed ingredients are lightly fermented and boiled for a long time in a large pot called a *sot* (솥).

Chapter V

Advice from a Silkworm

The Silkworm and Sun-hee looked at each other for some time in silence: at last the Silkworm took the opium pipe out of its mouth, and addressed her in a languid, sleepy voice.

"Who are *you?*" said the Silkworm.

This was not an encouraging opening for a conversation.

Sun-hee replied, rather shyly, "I—I hardly know, Sir, just at present—at least I know who I was when I got up this morning, but I think I must have changed several times since then."

"What do you mean by that?" said the Silkworm, sternly. "Explain yourself!"

"I ca'n't explain *myself*, I'm afraid, Sir," said Sun-hee, "because I'm not myself, you see."

"I don't see," said the Silkworm.

"I'm afraid I ca'n't put it more clearly," Sun-hee replied, very politely, "for I ca'n't understand it myself, to begin with; and being so many different sizes in a day is very confusing."

"It isn't," said the Silkworm.

"Well, perhaps you haven't found it so yet," said Sun-hee; "but when you have to turn into a chrysalis—you will some day, you know—and then after that into a moth, I should think you'll feel it a little queer, wo'n't you?"

"Not a bit," said the Silkworm.

"Well, perhaps *your* feelings may be different," said Sun-hee "all I know is, it would feel very queer to me."

"You!" said the Silkworm contemptuously. "Who are *you*?"

Which brought them back again to the beginning of the conversation. Sun-hee felt a little irritated at the Silkworm's making such very short remarks, and she drew herself up and said, very gravely, "I think you ought to tell me who *you* are, first."

"Why?" said the Silkworm.

Here was another puzzling question; and, as Sun-hee could not think of any good reason, and the Silkworm seemed to be in a very unpleasant state of mind, she turned away.

"Come back!" the Silkworm called after her. "I've something important to say!"

This sounded promising, certainly. Sun-hee turned and came back again.

"'Kick a stone in anger, and you will bruise your big toe,'" said the Silkworm.

"Is that all?" said Sun-hee, swallowing down her anger as well as she could.

"No," said the Silkworm.

Sun-hee thought she might as well wait, as she had nothing else to do, and perhaps after all it might tell her something worth hearing. For some time it puffed away without speaking; but at last it laid down its needle, took the opium pipe out of its mouth again, and said "So you think you're changed, do you?"

"I'm afraid I am, Sir," said Sun-hee. "I ca'n't remember things as I used—and I don't keep the same size even for a moment!"

"Ca'n't remember *what* things?" said the Silkworm.

"Well, I've tried to say '*How doth the mythical haetae*', but it all came different!" Sun-hee replied in a very melancholy voice.

"Repeat '*King Sejong*'," said the Silkworm.

Sun-hee folded her hands, and began:—

"Why, King Sejong, did you choose to invent Hangul
For women and children to abuse?
Your having done so has proved so cruel
To us Scholars, for whom heaven moved.
They no longer think that it's so strange,
That we can read the printed page!"

"That is not said right," said the Silkworm.

"Not quite right, I'm afraid," said Sun-hee, timidly: "Some of the words have got altered."

"It is wrong from beginning to end," said the Silkworm, decidedly; and there was silence for some time.

The Silkworm was the first to speak.

"What size do you want to be?" it asked.

"Oh, I'm not particular as to size," Sun-hee hastily replied; "Only one doesn't like changing so often, you know."

"I *don't* know," said the Silkworm.

Sun-hee said nothing: she had never been so much contradicted in all her life before, and she felt that she was losing her temper.

"Are you content now?" said the Silkworm.

"Well, I should like to be a little larger, Sir, if you wouldn't mind," said Sun-hee "to be no larger than a *jujube*[25] stone is a wretched size to be."

"It is a very good size indeed!" said the Silkworm angrily, rearing itself upright as it spoke (it was exactly the size of a *jujube* stone.)

"But I'm not used to it!" pleaded poor Sun-hee in a piteous tone. And she thought to herself "I wish the creatures wouldn't be so easily offended!"

"You'll get used to it in time," said the Silkworm; and it put the opium pipe into its mouth, and began smoking again.

This time Sun-hee waited patiently until it chose to speak again. In a short time the Silkworm took the opium pipe out of its mouth, and yawned once or twice, and shook itself. Then it got down from the embroidery frame, and crawled away into the grass, merely remarking, as it went, "One side will make you grow taller, and the other side will make you grow shorter."

"One side of *what*? The other side of *what*?" thought Sun-hee to herself.

"Of the mulberry leaf," said the Silkworm, just as if she had asked it aloud; and in another moment it was out of sight.

Sun-hee remained looking thoughtfully at the tree for a short time, wondering if perhaps he meant the *eum* and *yang*[26] of a leaf; "But how can I eat the top of the leaf without eating the bottom?" she said to herself. "Perhaps he meant the one side of the tree facing the sun and the other in shadow!" and, this making more sense, she stretched her arms out grabbing one leaf glowing with sunlight and, on the other side, one from

25 *jujube* stone—the pit of a southern Korean fruit (*Ziziphus jujuba*), also known as a Chinese date.

26 *eum* and *yang* (음양, [MR]*ŭm* and *yang*)—the Korean equivalent of *yin* and *yang*, representing the balance between good and evil, light and dark, and male and female.

the shade. But now when she looked down at the leaves in her hands, they both appeared the same.

"And now which is which?" she said to herself, and nibbled a little of the right-hand leaf to try the effect. The next moment she felt a violent blow underneath her chin: it had struck her foot!

She was a good deal frightened by this sudden change, but she felt there was no time to be lost, as she was shrinking rapidly: so she set to work at once to eat some of the other leaf. Her chin was pressed so closely against her foot, that there was hardly room to open her mouth; but she did it at last, and managed to swallow a bit of the left-hand leaf.

"Come, my head's free at last!" said Sun-hee in a tone of delight, which changed into alarm in another moment, when she found that her shoulders were nowhere to be found: all she could see, when she looked down, was an immense length of neck, which seemed to rise like a stalk out of a sea of green leaves that lay far below her.

"What *can* all that green stuff be?" said Sun-hee. "And where have my shoulders got to? An oh, my poor hands, how is it I ca'n't see you?" she was moving them about, as she spoke, but no result seemed to follow, except a little shaking among the distant green leaves.

As there seemed to be no chance of getting her hands up to her head, she tried to get her head down to *them*, and was delighted to find that her neck would bend about easily in any direction, like a serpent. She had just succeeded in curving it down into a graceful *eum-yang,* and was going to dive into the leaves, which she found to be nothing but the tops of the trees under which she had been wandering, when a sharp hiss made her draw back in a hurry: a large magpie had flown into her face, and was beating her violently with its wings.

"Serpent!" screamed the Magpie.

"I'm *not* a serpent!" said Sun-hee indignantly. "Let me alone!"

"Serpent, I say again!" repeated the Magpie, but in a more subdued tone, and added, with a kind of sob, "I've tried every way, but nothing seems to suit them!"

"I haven't the least idea what you're talking about," said Sun-hee.

"I've tried the roots of trees, and I've tried banks, and I've tried hedges," the Magpie went on, without attending to her; "but those serpents! There's no pleasing them!"

Sun-hee was more and more puzzled, but she thought there was no use in saying anything more until the Magpie had finished.

"As if it wasn't trouble enough hatching the eggs," said the Magpie; "but I must be on the look-out for serpents, night and day! Why, I haven't had a wink of sleep!"

"I'm very sorry you've been annoyed," said Sun-hee, who was beginning to see its meaning.

"And just as I'd taken the highest tree in the wood," continued the Magpie, raising its voice to a shriek, "and just as I was thinking I should be free of them at last, they come wriggling down from the sky! Ugh, Serpent!"

"But I'm *not* a serpent, I tell you!" said Sun-hee, "I'm a little girl—"

"'When a rotten egg crows at dawn'!" said the Magpie, in a tone of the deepest contempt. "I've seen a good many little girls in my time, but never *one* with such a neck as that! No, no! You're a serpent; and there's no use denying it. I suppose you'll be telling me next that you never tasted an egg!"

"I *have* tasted eggs, certainly," said Sun-hee, who was a very truthful child; "but little girls eat eggs quite as much as serpents do, you know."

"I don't believe it," said the Magpie: "but if they do, then they're a kind of serpent: that's all I can say."

This was such a new idea to Sun-hee, that she was quite silent for a minute or two, which gave the Magpie the opportunity of adding, "You're looking for eggs, I know *that* well enough; and what does it matter to me whether you're a little girl or a serpent?"

"It matters a good deal to *me*," said Sun-hee hastily; "but I'm not looking for eggs, as it happens; and, if I was, I shouldn't want *yours*: I'd expect to bite into a bone!"

"Well, be off, then!" said the Magpie in a sulky tone, as it settled down again into its nest. Sun-hee crouched down among the trees as well as she could, for her neck kept getting entangled among the branches, and every now and then she had to stop and untwist it. After a while she remembered that she still held the leaves in her hands, and she set to work very carefully, nibbling first at one and then at the other, and growing sometimes shorter, until she had succeeded in bringing herself down to her usual height.

It was so long since she had been anything near the right size, that it felt quite strange at first; but she got used to it in a few minutes, and began talking to herself, as usual, "come, there's half my plan done now! How puzzling all these changes are! I'm never sure what I'm going to be, from one minute to another! However, I've got back to my right size: the next thing is, to get into that beautiful secret garden—how *is* that to be done, I wonder?" As she said this, she came suddenly upon an open place, with a little house in it surrounded by a little wall and gate. The house was only about as tall as a cow. "Whoever lives there," thought Sun-hee, "it'll never do to come upon them *this* size: why, I should frighten them out of their wits!" So she began nibbling at the righthand leaf again, and did not venture to go near the gate till she had brought herself down to about the size of a chicken.

Chapter VI

Pig and Red Pepper

For a moment or two she stood looking at the house, and wondering what to do next, when suddenly a soldier in a *gwanbok*[27] came running from behind the wall—(she considered him to be a soldier because he was in a *gwanbok* and because this house, with golden chrysanthemum and bamboo ornaments on its gates, must belong to someone noble: otherwise, judging by his long face only, she would have called him a squid)—and rapped loudly at the gate. It was opened by another soldier in a *gwanbok,* with a rather bulbous head, and small eyes like an octopus; and both soldiers had long, wavy arms that curled all around them. She felt very curious to know what it was all about, and crept a little way out of the wood to listen.

The Squid-Soldier began by producing a great scroll, stuck to one of the cups on the end of one of his tentacles. He handed this over to the other, saying, in a solemn tone, "For Concubine Ok-baem. An invitation from the Queen of *Hwatu*[28] to play *yut*."[29] The Octopus-Soldier repeated, in the

27 *gwanbok* (관복, [MR]*kwanbok*)—the formal, courtly attire of a soldier.
28 *hwatu* (화투, [MR]*hwat'u*)—a Korean card game, played with a deck of 48 cards.

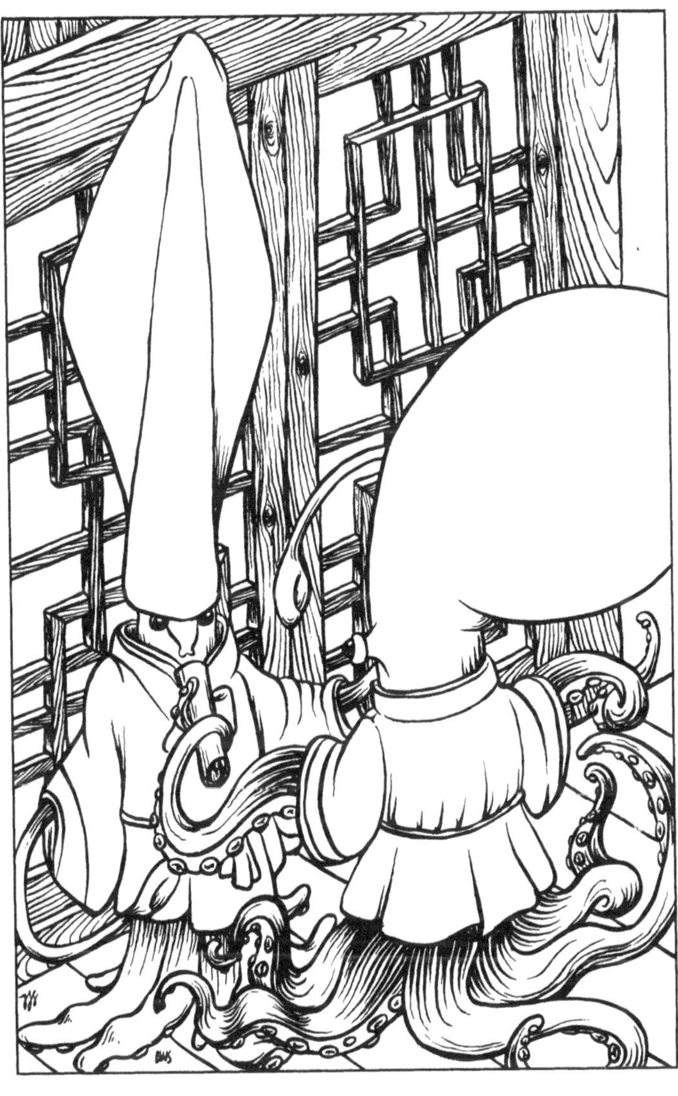

comprising 12 suits, one for each month of the year, each with a design of highly stylized flowers representative of the month. The game is also colled *Go-Stop* (고스톱), *goseutop*) and *Godori* (고도리), but the name of the cards

same solemn tone, only changing the order of the words a little, "From the Queen of *Hwatu.* An invitation for Concubine Ok-baem to play *yut*."

Then they both bowed, and their tentacles got entangled together.

Sun-hee laughed so much at this that she had to run back into the wood for fear of their hearing her; and, when she next peeped out, the Squid-Soldier was gone, and the other was sitting on the ground near the gate, his eyes, extended from little stalks at the side of his head, were stupidly staring at each other.

Sun-hee went timidly up to the gate, and knocked.

"There's no sort of use in knocking," said the Soldier, "and that for two reasons. First, because I'm on the same side of the gate as you are: secondly, because they're making such a noise inside, no one could possibly hear you." And certainly there was a most extraordinary noise going on within—a constant howling and sniffling, and every now and then a great crash, as if a pot or bowl had been broken to pieces.

"Please, then," said Sun-hee, "how am I to get in?"

"There might be some sense in your knocking," the Soldier went on, without attending to her, "if we had the gate between us. For instance, if you were *inside*, you might knock, and I could let you out, you know." He was looking at himself all the time he was speaking, and this Sun-hee thought decidedly uncivil. "But perhaps he ca'n't help it," she said to herself: "his eyelids are so *very* outstretched. But at any rate he might answer questions—How am I to get in?" she repeated, aloud.

"I shall sit here," the Soldier remarked, "till tomorrow—"

used to play the game as well as of the winning move is *hwatu*.

29 *yut* (윷, also 윷놀이 *yunnori*)—a traditional Korean game, played by tossing four small sticks, round on one side and flat on the other, thrown like dice, How the sticks land (flat or round side up) determines the number of moves which a player may move his counter along a circular course marked on either a board or simply scratched on the ground.

At this moment the gate opened, and a large gourd came skimming out, straight at the Soldier's head: it just grazed him, and rolled off into the trees.

"—or next day, maybe," the Soldier continued in the same tone, exactly as if nothing had happened.

"How am I to get in?" asked Sun-hee again, in a louder tone.

"*Are* you to get in at all?" said the Soldier. "That's the first question, you know."

It was, no doubt: only Sun-hee did not like to be told so. "It's really dreadful," she muttered to herself, "the way all the creatures argue. It's enough to drive one crazy!"

The Soldier seemed to think this a good opportunity for repeating his remark, with variations. "I shall sit here," he said, "on and off, for days and days."

"But what am *I* to do?" said Sun-hee.

"Anything you like," said the Soldier, and began whistling.

"Oh, there's no use in talking to him," said Sun-hee desperately: "he's perfectly idiotic!" And she opened the gate and went through the courtyard and slid open one of the doors.

This door led right into a long kitchen, which was full of smoke from one end to the other: Concubine Ok-baem was sitting on a large cushioned chair in the middle, nursing a baby: the cook was leaning over the fire, stirring a large pot which seemed to be full of soup.

"There's certainly too much red pepper in that soup!" Sun-hee said to herself, as well as she could for wiping the tears from her eyes.

There was certainly too much of it in the *air*. Even Concubine Ok-baem sniffled occasionally; and as for the baby, it was sniffling and howling alternately without a moment's pause. The only two creatures in the kitchen, whose eyes *weren't* watering or nose running, were the cook, and a large

tiger, which was perched on the back of Concubine Ok-baem's chair and grinning from ear to ear.

"Please would you tell me," said Sun-hee, a little timidly, for she was not quite sure whether it was good manners for her to speak first, "why your tiger grins like that?"

"It's a Temple-Tiger," said Concubine Ok-baem, "and that's why. Pig!"

She said the last word with such violence that Sun-hee quite jumped; but she saw in another moment that it was addressed to the baby, and not to her, so she took courage, and went on again:—

"I didn't know that Temple-Tigers always grinned; in fact, I didn't know that tigers *could* grin."

"They all can," said Concubine Ok-baem; "and most of them do."

"I don't know of any that do," Sun-hee said very politely, feeling quite pleased to have got into a conversation.

"You don't know much," said Concubine Ok-baem, "and that's a fact."

Sun-hee did not at all like the tone of this remark, and thought it would be as well to introduce some other subject of conversation. While she was trying to fix on one, the cook took the pot of soup off the fire and at once set to work throwing everything within her reach at Concubine Ok-baem and the baby—the kettle came first; then followed a shower of pots, bowls, and baskets. Concubine Ok-baem took no notice of them even when they hit her; and the baby was howling so much already, that it was quite impossible to say whether the blows hurt it or not.

"Oh, *please* mind what you're doing!" cried Sun-hee, jumping up and down in an agony of terror. "Oh, there goes his precious nose!" as an unusually large bowl flew close by it, and very nearly carried it off.

"If everybody minded their own business," Concubine Ok-baem said, in a hoarse growl, "I could get this baby fed and then have a few moments to learn how to do a brush painting to hang on that wall;" she pointed to a small wall near the door that was covered with bits of red pepper and cabbage.

"That *wouldn't* be possible," said Sun-hee, who felt very glad to get an opportunity of showing off a little of her knowledge. "It takes years of study and patience to learn brush painting; a person may do thousands of paintings before doing one worthy of being signed with a chop and hanging on a wall."

"Talking of chops," said Concubine Ok-baem, "chop off her head!"

Sun-hee glanced rather anxiously at the cook, to see if she meant to take the hint; but the cook was busily stirring the soup, and seemed not to be listening, so she went on again: "First you learn to paint orchids I *think*; or is it bamboo?"

"Oh, don't bother *me*!" said Concubine Ok-baem. "I don't care to hear what knowledge you've gained from listening at screen doors!" And with that she began nursing her child again, singing a sort of lullaby to it as she did so, and giving it a violent shake at the end of every line:—

> "*Round prince, round prince, grow pig, grow pig,*
> *Whichever side you suckle, grow pig.*"[30]

While Ok-baem sang the song, she kept tossing the baby violently up and down, and the poor little thing howled so, that Sun-hee could hardly hear the words.

"Here! 'Take a homely baby into your arms' and nurse it a bit, if you like!" Concubine Ok-baem said to Sun-hee, flinging the baby at her as she spoke. "I must go and get ready to play *yut* with the Queen of *Hwatu*, and she hurried out of the room.

30 This poem parodies a traditional lullaby as transcribed by Cho Dong-il, 1966, "Round quince, round quince..." See *Humor in Korean Litueature*, Si-sa-yong-osa, Seoul, 1982.

The cook threw a gourd after her as she went, but it just missed her.

Sun-hee caught the baby with some difficulty, as it was a queer-shaped little creature, and held out its arms and legs in all directions, "just like a star-fish," thought Sun-hee. The poor little thing was snorting like an ill-tempered ox when she caught it, and kept doubling itself up and straightening itself out again, so that altogether, for the first minute or two, it was as much as she could do to hold it.

As soon as she had made out the proper way of nursing it (which was to twist it up into a sort of knot, and then keep tight hold of its right ear and left foot, so as to prevent its undoing itself), she carried it out into the open air. "If I don't take this child away with me," thought Sun-hee, "they're sure to kill it in a day or two. Wouldn't it be murder to leave it behind?" She said the last words out loud, and the little thing grunted in reply (it had left off sniffling by this time). "Don't grunt," said Sun-hee; "that's not at all a proper way of expressing yourself."

The baby grunted again, and Sun-hee looked very anxiously into its face to see what was the matter with it. There could be no doubt that it had a *very* turn-up nose, much more like a snout than a real nose: also its eyes were getting extremely small for a baby: altogether Sun-hee did not at like the look of the thing at all. "But perhaps it was only sobbing," she thought, and looked into its eyes again, to see if there were any tears.

No, there were no tears. "If you're going to turn into a pig, my dear," said Sun-hee, seriously, "I'll have nothing more to do with you. Mind now!" The poor little thing sobbed again (or grunted, it was impossible to say which), and they went on for some while in silence.

Sun-hee was just beginning to think to herself, "Now, what am I to do with this creature, when I get it home?" when it

grunted again, so violently, that she looked down into its face in some alarm. This time there could be no mistake about it: it was neither more nor less than a pig, and she felt that it would be quite absurd for her to carry it any further.

So she set the little creature down, and felt quite relieved to see it trot through the gate and quietly into the wood. "If it had grown up," she said to herself, "it would have made a dreadfully ugly child: but it makes rather a handsome pig, I think."

Walking along through the wood, she saw a swing hanging from the bough of a tree and decided to sit down and cool herself, as she was still suffering from the stifling heat of Concubine Ok-baem's kitchen. She began thinking over other children she knew, who might do very well as pigs, and was just saying to herself, "if one only knew the right way to change them—" when she was a little startled by seeing Father Sanshin[31] sitting on a pile of rocks a short distance away. Seeing that he was sitting quietly, she dared not make a sound and disturb his meditation: and as she watched him, it occurred to her that his tiger was nowhere to be seen. "I wonder where his tiger has got off to—" she said softly to herself as she leaned back. "'Speak of the tiger and see his stripes'!" she exclaimed, for there above her head, sitting on a bough of the tree, was the Temple-Tiger.

The Temple-Tiger only grinned when it saw Sun-hee. It looked good-natured, she thought: still it had very long claws and a great many teeth, so she felt that it ought to be treated with respect.

"Mountain Spirit," she began, rather timidly, as she did not at all know whether it would like the name: however, it only grinned a little wider. "Come, it's pleased so far," thought

31 Father Sanshin—a shamanistic spirit, also known as the Mountain Spirit, usually depicted as an old man with a tiger reclining at or about his feet, whose image is often enshrined in a small building near the forest at the back of Buddhist temples.

Sun-hee, and she went on. "Would you tell me, please, which way I ought to go from here?"

"That depends a good deal on where you want to get to," said the Tiger.

"I don't much care where—" said Sun-hee.

"Then it doesn't matter which way you go," said the Tiger.

"—so long as I get *somewhere*," Sun-hee added as an explanation.

"Oh, you're sure to do that," said the Tiger, "if you only walk long enough."

Sun-hee felt that this could not be denied, so she tried another question. "What sort of people live about here?"

"In *that* direction," the Tiger said, waving its right paw round, "lives a Scholar: and in *that* direction," waving the other paw, "lives a Masked Hare. Visit either you like: they're both mad."

"But I don't want to go among mad people," Sun-hee remarked.

"Oh, you ca'n't help that," said the Tiger: "we're all mad here. I'm mad. You're mad."

"How do you know I'm mad?" said Sun-hee.

"You must be," said the Tiger, "or you wouldn't have come here."

Sun-hee didn't think that proved it at all: however, she went on: "And how do you know that you're mad?"

"To begin with," said the Tiger, "a dog's not mad. You grant that?"

"I suppose so," said Sun-hee.

"Well, then," the Tiger went on, "you see a dog growls when it's angry, and wags its tail when it's pleased. Now *I* growl when I'm pleased, and wag my tail when I'm angry. Therefore I'm mad."

"*I* call it purring, now growling," said Sun-hee.

"Call it what you like," said the Tiger. "Do you play *yut* with the Queen of *Hwatu* to-day?"

"What?" asked Sun-hee.

"No," said the Tiger impatiently, *"Hwatu;* it isn't nice of you to be disrespectful!"

"I'm terribly sorry," said Sun-hee, not really sure what she had done.

"You'll see me there," said the Tiger, and vanished.

Sun-hee was not much surprised at this, she was getting so well used to queer things happening. While she was still looking at the place where it had been, it suddenly appeared again.

"By-the-bye, what became of the baby?" said the Tiger. "I'd nearly forgotten to ask."

"It turned into a pig," Sun-hee answered very quietly, just as if the Tiger had come back in a natural way.

"I thought it would," said the Tiger, and vanished again.

Sun-hee waited a little, half expecting to see it again, but it did not appear, and after a minute or two she walked on in the direction in which the Masked Hare was said to live. "I've seen scholars before," she said to herself: "the Masked Hare will be much the most interesting, and perhaps, since I'm unlikely to see a goblin in broad daylight, perhaps it wo'n't be raving mad." As she said this, she looked up, and there was the Tiger again, sitting on a branch of a tree.

"Did you say 'pig', or 'twig'?" said the Tiger.

"I said 'pig'," replied Sun-hee; "and I wish you wouldn't keep appearing and vanishing so suddenly: you make one quite giddy!"

"All right," said the Tiger; and this time it vanished quite slowly, beginning with the end of the tail, and ending with the grin, which remained some time after the rest of it had gone.

"Well! I've heard of 'losing face' before," thought Sun-hee but I've never seen it actually happen! This Tiger has lost everything but his grin! It's the most curious thing I ever saw in all my life!"

She had not gone much farther before she came in sight of the house of the Masked Hare: she thought it must be the right house, because the chimneys were shaped like ears and the roof was thatched with fur. It was so large a house, that she did not like to go nearer till she had nibbled some more of the left-hand leaf, and raised herself to about the height of a goat: even then she walked up towards it rather timidly, saying to herself "Suppose it should be raving mad after all! I almost wish I'd gone to see the Scholar instead!"

Chapter VII

A Mad Ginseng-Party

There was a low platform set out under a tree in front of the house, and the Masked Hare and the Scholar were having ginseng tea on it: a large ginseng root was sitting between them and the other two were using it as a cushion, resting their elbows on it, and talking over its head. "Very uncomfortable for the ginseng," thought Sun-hee; "only as it's a root, I suppose it doesn't have a mind to mind."

The platform was a large one, but the three were all crowded together at one corner of it. "No room! No room!" they cried out when they saw Sun-hee coming. "There's plenty of room!" said Sun-hee indignantly, and she sat down on a corner at one end of the platform.

"Have some *makkolli*, the Masked Hare said in an encouraging tone.

Sun-hee looked all round the table, but there was nothing on it but tea. "I don't see any *makkolli*," she remarked.

"There isn't any," said the Masked Hare.

"Then it wasn't very civil of you to offer it," said Sun-hee angrily.

"It wasn't very civil of you to sit down when you weren't invited," said the Masked Hare.

"I didn't know it was *your* platform," said Sun-hee: "it has room for a great many more than three."

"You hair wants cutting," said the Scholar. He had been staring at Sun-hee for some time with great curiosity, and this was his first speech.

"You should learn not to stare and not to make personal remarks," Sun-hee said with some severity: "it's very rude."

The Scholar opened his eyes very wide and giggled on hearing this; but all he *said* was "Why is a crow like a scholar's desk?"

"Come, we shall have some fun now!" thought Sun-hee. "I'm glad they've begun asking riddles—I believe I can guess that," she added aloud.

"Do you mean that you think you can find out the answer to it?" said the Masked Hare.

"Exactly so," said Sun-hee.

"Then you should say what you mean," the Masked Hare went on.

"I do," Sun-hee hastily replied; "at least—at least I mean what I say—that's the same thing, you know."

"Not the same thing a bit!" said the Scholar. "Why, you might just as well say that 'I see what I eat' is the same thing as 'I eat what I see'!"

"You might just as well say," added the Ginseng, which seemed to be talking in its sleep, "that 'I breathe when I sleep' is the same thing as 'I sleep when I breathe'!"

"It is the same thing with you," said the Scholar, and here the conversation dropped, and the party sat silent for a minute, and Sun-hee thought over all she could remember about crows and scholar's desks, which wasn't much.

The Scholar was the first to break the silence. "What day of the lunar month is it?" he said, turning to Sun-hee: he had taken a moon clock out of his pocket, and was looking at it uneasily, turning it this way and that in the sunlight.

Sun-hee considered a little, and then said, "The sixth."

"Two days wrong!" sighed the Scholar. "A lunar clock only works at night! What's the use of it in the daylight?" he added, looking angrily at the Masked Hare.

"Wait till the sun has gone behind a cloud, that may work," the Masked Hare suggested meekly. It didn't seem to help.

"I ca'n't wait until night, when the moon is full to find out what day it is," the Scholar grumbled: "you shouldn't have gotten me a lunar clock!"

The Masked Hare took the moon clock and looked at it gloomily: then he dipped it into his cup of tea, and looked at it again; but he could think of nothing better to say than to expand on his first remark, "It should work on *partly* cloudy days—"

Sun-hee had been looking over his shoulder with some curiosity. "What a funny clock!" she remarked to the Masked Hare. "And his hat is unusual as well—it's a Confucian design, though quite the large size, isn't it?"

"Not precisely," said the Masked Hare, "it's a Confusion hat, which is quite different."

"It's what makes him raving don't you know," the Masked Hare whispered to Sun-hee.

"Then why doesn't he just take it off?" she asked.

"The butterflies would get out, of course!" the Ginseng said in a shocked whisper, "that's why it's so large, it's where he keeps them."

"Oh, I am confused," moaned Sun-hee.

"Give her a hat!" screamed the Masked Hare. "You ca'n't study Confusionism unless you have a hat! Ginseng! Find a hat for her, quickly!"

"Oh, please," begged Sun-hee, "I really don't want one." She should not have worried, for no sooner had she spoken these words, than the Ginseng had fallen asleep again, and the whole subject was forgotten.

"I'm getting tired of this," the Masked Hare said, yawning. "I vote the young lady tells us a story."

"'When the tiger is not about, the hare behaves like the King'," Sun-hee thought to herself, and wondered momentarily where the Temple-Tiger had got off to. "I'm afraid I don't know one," she said, rather alarmed at the proposal.

"Then the Ginseng shall!" they both cried. "Wake up, Ginseng!" And they pulled at its roots on both sides at once.

The Ginseng slowly opened its eyes. "I wasn't asleep," it said in a hoarse, feeble voice, "I heard every word you fellows were saying."

"Tell us a story!" said the Masked Hare.

"Yes, please do!" pleaded Sun-hee.

"And be quick about it," added the Scholar, "or you'll be asleep again before it's done."

"When tigers smoked long pipes, there lived three friends," the Ginseng began in a great hurry; "a cricket, an ant, and a kingfisher.[32] and as it was the ant's birthday, he wanted to have a feast—"

"What did they feast on?" said Sun-hee, who always took a great interest in eating and drinking.

"They feasted on fish," said the Ginseng, after thinking a minute or two.

"The cricket couldn't have done that, you know," Sun-hee gently remarked. "Fish eat crickets."

"And so it did," said the Ginseng.

"If you already know this story," the Masked Hare retorted, "why don't you finish it yourself!"

32 kingfisher—The story described is a traditional Korean folktale explaining why the cricket has a bare forehead, the ant a thin waist, and the kingfisher a long beak.

"No, please go on!" Sun-hee said very humbly. "I wo'n't interrupt again. I dare say there must be more—"

"More, indeed!" said the Ginseng indignantly. "And so the ant and kingfisher—they went fishing, you know—"

"Why did they go fishing?" said Sun-hee, quite forgetting her promise.

"Because the cricket was getting very hot inside the fish's stomach," answered the Ginseng, "and he had already lost part of his forehead."

"I want a clean cup," interrupted the Scholar: "let's all move one place on."

He moved as he spoke, and the Ginseng followed him: the Masked Hare moved into the Ginseng's place, and Sun-hee rather unwillingly took the place of the Masked Hare.

Sun-hee did not wish to offend the Ginseng again, so she began very cautiously: "But I don't understand. How did it help the cricket for the kingfisher and ant to go fishing?"

"Why, the kingfisher caught the fish that had swallowed the cricket and cut him out," said the Scholar; "and that's why the ant's waist is so tiny and the kingfisher's beak so long."

"But why should that happen?" Sun-hee said to the Ginseng, not being able to understand this last remark.

"Because it was so funny!" said the Ginseng.

This answer so confused poor Sun-hee, that she let the Ginseng, Masked Hare, and Scholar go on laughing for some time without interrupting.

After a time the Ginseng had closed its eyes and was going off into a doze. Sun-hee turned to the Scholar and said quietly, "About the Ginseng's story—I really don't think—"

"Then you shouldn't talk," said the Scholar.

This piece of rudeness was more than Sun-hee could bear: she got up in great disgust, and walked off: the Ginseng fell asleep instantly, and neither of the others took the least notice of her going, though she looked back once or twice, half hoping that they would call after her: the last time she saw them, they were trying to put the Ginseng into the teapot.

"At any rate I'll never go there again!" said Sun-hee, as she picked her way through the wood. "It's the stupidest teaparty I ever was at in all my life!"

Just as she said this, she noticed that one of the trees had a door leading right into it. "That's very curious!" she thought. "But everything's curious today. I think I may as well go in at once." And in she went.

Once more she found herself in the long alley, and close to the scholar's desk. "Now, I'll manage better this time," she said to herself, and began by taking the little brass key, and unlocking the door that led into the secret garden. Then she set to work nibbling at one of the mulberry leaves (she had kept one in her pocket) till she was about as high as a cat; then she walked down the little passage: and then—she found herself at last in the beautiful secret garden, among the bright orchids, lotus blossoms, and cool reflecting ponds.

Chapter VIII

The Queen of *Hwatu*'s Yut-Ground

A huge Rose of Sharon[33] stood near the entrance of the garden: the blossoms growing on it were white, but there were three gardeners on it, busily painting them a bright pink. Sun-hee thought this a very curious thing, and she went nearer to watch them, and, just as she came up to them, she heard one of them say "Look out now, June! Don't go splashing paint over me like that!"

"I couldn't help it," said June, in a sulky tone. "November jogged my elbow."

On which November looked up and said "That's right, June! Always lay the blame on others!"

"You'd better not talk!" said June. "I heard the Queen of *Hwatu* say only yesterday you deserved to be beheaded."

"What for?" said the one who had spoken first.

33 Rose of Sharon (무궁화, *mugunghwa*, *Hibiscus syriacus*)—the national flower of Korea.

"That's none of your business, December!" said November.

"Yes, it is his business!" said June. "And I'll tell him—it was for bringing the cook seaweed instead of garlic."

November flung down his brush, and had just begun "Well, of all the unjust things—" when his eye chanced to fall upon Sun-hee, as she stood watching them, and he checked himself suddenly: the others looked round also, and all of them bowed low.

"Would you tell me, please," said Sun-hee, a little timidly, "why you are painting those blossoms pink?"

June and November said nothing, but looked at December. December began, in a low voice, "Why, the fact is, you see, Miss, this here ought to have been a *pink* Rose of Sharon, and we put a white one in by mistake; and, if the Queen of *Hwatu* was to find it out, we should all have our heads cut off, you know. So you see, Miss, we're doing our best, before she comes, to—" At this moment, June, who had been anxiously looking across the garden, called out "The Queen! The Queen!" and the three gardeners instantly threw themselves flat upon their faces, There was a sound of many footsteps. and Sun-hee looked round, eager to see the Queen of *Hwatu*.

First came twelve soldiers ornamented with flowers and all carrying chrysanthemums: they too were card-shaped like the three gardeners, oblong and flat, with their arms and legs at the corners: next came twelve courtiers: these were ornamented all over with flags and floral designs, and walked two and two, as the soldiers did. After these came the royal children: merrily along, hand-in-hand, in couples: they were all ornamented with birds and flowers. Next came the guests, mostly Kings and Queens ornamented with a special circular design, and among them Sun-hee recognized the White Rabbit: it was talking in a hurried manner, giggling nervously at everything that was said as if embarrassed, and he went by without noticing her. Then followed the Prince of *Hwatu*, and, last of all in this grand procession, came THE KING AND QUEEN OF *HWATU*.

Sun-hee was rather doubtful whether she ought not to lie down on her face like the three gardeners, but she could not remember every having heard of such a rule at processions; "and besides, what would be the use of a procession," thought she, "if people had all to lie down on their faces, so that they couldn't see it?" So she stood where she was, and waited.

When the procession came opposite to Sun-hee, they all stopped and stared at her, and the Queen said, severely, 'Who is this?" She said it to the Prince of *Hwatu*, who only bowed and laughed nervously in reply.

"Idiot!" said the Queen, tossing her head impatiently; and, turning to Sun-hee, she went on: "What's your name, child?"

"My name is An Sun-hee, so please your Majesty," said Sun-hee very politely; but she added, to herself, "Why, they're only a pack of cards, after all. I needn't be afraid of them!"

"And who are *these*?" said the Queen, pointing to the three gardeners who were lying round the Rose of Sharon, for, you see, as they were lying on their faces, and the pattern on their backs was the same as the rest of the pack, she could not tell whether they were gardeners, or soldiers, or courtiers, or three of her own children.

"How should *I* know?" said Sun-hee, surprised at her own courage. "It's no business of *mine*."

The Queen turned crimson with fury, and, after glaring at her for a moment like a wild beast, began screaming "Off with her head! Off with—"

"Nonsense! 'Draw a sword at the sound of a mosquito!'" said Sun-hee, very loudly and decidedly, and the Queen was silent.

The King laid his hand upon her arm, and timidly said "'A whelp doesn't know enough to fear the tiger's grin'!"

The Queen turned angrily away from him, and said to the Prince "Turn them over!"

The Prince did so, very carefully, with one foot.

"Get up!" said the Queen in a shrill, loud voice, and the three gardeners instantly jumped up, and began bowing to the King, the Queen, the royal children, and everybody else.

"Leave off that!" screamed the Queen. "You make me giddy." And then, turning to the Rose of Sharon, she went on "What *have* you been doing here?"

"May it please your Majesty," said December, in a very humble tone, going down on one knee as he spoke, "we were trying—"

"*I* see!" said the Queen, who had meanwhile been examining the blossoms. "Off with their heads!" and the procession moved on, three of the soldiers remaining behind to execute the unfortunate gardeners, who ran to Sun-hee for protection.

"You shall not be beheaded!" said Sun-hee, and she put them into a large flower-arranging bowl that stood near. The three soldiers wandered about for a minute or two, looking for them, and then quietly marched off after the others.

"Are their heads off?" shouted the Queen of *Hwatu*.

"Their heads are gone, if it please your Majesty!" the soldiers shouted in reply.

"That's right!" shouted the Queen. "Can you play *yut*?"

The soldiers were silent, and looked at Sun-hee, as the question was evidently meant for her.

"Yes!" shouted Sun-hee.

"Come on, then!" roared the Queen, and Sun-hee joined the procession, wondering very much what would happen next.

Sun-hee thought she had never seen such a curious *yut*-ground in her life: it was set outside the main gate of the palace: the *yut* sticks were snakes, and the pebbles were actually clams, which tended to bury themselves in the sand.

Sun-hee watched the King and Queen of *Hwatu* take their turns first, of course, and noticed that the snakes remained rigid when tossed, and always landed round side up, in order

to afford the most points. However, when it came to her turn, and she tossed them into the air, they wriggled and squirmed until they were most dreadfully tangled. Sun-hee could not help but laugh at this strange disadvantage, and managed to unsnarl them enough to throw again with slightly better results. She was trying to count her points, and it was very provoking to find that the clams kept disappearing into the sand, which made her lose count: besides all this, the snakes were wriggling about from one side to another, so that they had soon become entangled again.

The Queen, disturbed at how long it was taking Sun-hee to finish her turn, decided she must be cheating and shouted "Off with her head!" Sun-hee began to feel very uneasy: to be sure, she had not as yet had any dispute with the Queen, but just then one of the soldiers, tripping over several of the clams that had resurfaced, tottered over, spilling the barley water he was carrying onto the Queen. "Off with his head!" the Queen bellowed.

"It will dry, dear," said the trembling King, trying to pacify his wife.

"'Hang a straw door on iron hinges'," whispered Concubine Ok-baem to Sun-hee.

"You are now under sentence of execution madame!" the Queen of *Hwatu* yelled, pointing her finger. Sun-hee could not tell if it was she or Concubine Ok-baem the Queen of *Hwatu* was pointing to, and began looking for some way of escape.

"How are you getting on?" said the Temple-Tiger whose wide grin had suddenly appeared.

Sun-hee waited till the eyes appeared, and then nodded. "It's no use speaking to it," she thought, "till its ears have come, or at least one of them." In another moment the whole head appeared, and then Sun-hee put down the *yut* snake, and began an account of the game. The tiger seemed to think that there was enough of it now in sight, and no more of it appeared

"Who *are* you talking to?" said the King, coming up to Sun-hee, and looking at the Tiger's head with great curiosity.

"It's a friend of mine—a Temple-Tiger," said Sun-hee: "allow me to introduce it."

"I don't like the look of it at all," said the King: "however, it may kowtow to me, if it likes."

"I'd rather not," the Tiger remarked.

"Don't be impertinent," said the King, "and don't look at me like that!" He got behind Sun-hee as he spoke.

"'A mouse before a tiger'," thought Sun-hee.

"Well, it must be removed," said the King very decidedly; and he called to the Queen, who was passing at the moment, "My dear! I wish you would have this Tiger removed!"

The Queen had only one way of settling all difficulties, great or small. "Off with his head!" she said without even looking around.

In a few moments the executioner and a large crowd had collected round the Tiger: there was a dispute going on between the executioner, the King, and the Queen who were all talking at once.

Sun-hee was appealed to by all three to settle the question, and they repeated their arguments to her, though, as they all spoke at once, she found it very hard to make out exactly what they said.

The executioner's argument was, that you couldn't cut off a head unless there was a body to cut if off from: that he had never had to do such a thing before, and he wasn't going to begin at his time of life.

The King's argument was that anything that had a head could be beheaded, and that you weren't to talk nonsense.

The Queen's argument was that, if something wasn't done about it in less than no time, she'd have everybody executed, all round. (This last remark made the whole party look rather uncomfortable.)

Sun-hee could think of nothing else to say but "It belongs to Concubine Ok-baem: you'd better ask *her* about it."

"She's in prison," the Queen said to the executioner: "fetch her here." And the executioner went off like an arrow.

The Tiger's head began fading away the moment he was gone, and, by the time he had come back with Concubine Ok-baem, it had entirely disappeared: "Tie a gong on the neck of that Tiger.'" yelled the King as he and the executioner ran wildly up and down, looking for it, while the rest of the party went back to the game.

CHAPTER IX

The Mock Turtleboat's Story

"You ca'n't think how glad I am to see you again, you dear old thing!" said Concubine Ok-baem, as she tucked her arm affectionately into Sun-hee's, and they walked off together.

Sun-hee was very glad to find her in such a pleasant temper, and thought to herself that perhaps it was only the red pepper that had made her so savage when they met in the kitchen.

"When I'm a Queen," she said to herself (not in a very hopeful tone, though), "I wo'n't have any red pepper in my kitchen at all. Soup does very well without—Maybe it's always red pepper that makes people hot-tempered." she went on, very much pleased at having found out a new kind of rule, "and vinegar that makes them sour—and greens that makes them bitter—and—and bean paste with sugar and such things that make children sweet-tempered. I only wish people knew that: then they wouldn't be so stingy about it, you know—"

She had quite forgotten Concubine Ok-baem by this time, and was a little startled when she heard her voice close to her ear. "You're thinking about something, my dear, and that makes you forget to talk. I ca'n't tell you just now what the moral of that is, but I shall remember it in a bit."

"Perhaps it hasn't one," Sun-hee ventured to remark.

"*Aigo,* child!" said Concubine Ok-baem. "Everything's got a moral, if only you can find it." And she squeezed herself up close to Sun-hee's side as she spoke.

Sun-hee found it difficult keeping close to her: first because Concubine Ok-baem's *chima*[34] was very round; and secondly, because she was exactly the right height to allow the long ornamental pin in Concubine Ok-baem's hair to jab her uncomfortably in the ear. However, she did not like to be rude: so she bore it as well as she could.

"I hope I can remember how to play this game well," she said, by way of keeping up the conversation a little.

"You ca'n't expect to win," said Concubine Ok-baem: and the moral of that is—"'Knowledge is power'."

"And how would it be clever if I were to lose?" asked Sun-hee.

"You're playing the Queen of *Hwatu* aren't you?" replied Ok-baem.

Sun-hee considered this and decided that Concubine Ok-baem was most probably right. "How fond she is of finding morals in things!" Sun-hee thought to herself.

"I dare say you're wondering why I don't put my arm round your waist," Concubine Ok-baem said, after a pause: "the reason is, that I'm doubtful about the temper of your *yut* snake. Shall I try the experiment?"

"He might bite," Sun-hee cautiously replied, not feeling at all anxious to have the experiment tried.

34 *chima* (치마, [MR]*ch'ima*)—the wide skirt of the traditional woman's dress, or *hanbok* (한복).

"Very true," said Concubine Ok-baem: snakes and mothers-in-law both bite. And the moral of that is—"'A brown dog takes sides with a pig'."

"Only mothers-in-law don't really bite," Sun-hee remarked.

"'Knowledge is sickness'," said Ok-baem grimacing.

"I beg your pardon," replied Sun-hee, "but previously you said that 'knowledge is power'."

"'No sooner does man's wisdom grow with age, than he becomes like a child'," said Concubine Ok-baem: or if you prefer—'Leave a strawberry and eat a pumpkin'—or, if you'd like it more simply—'You have more to lose if you had gained more in the first place so that small thoughts are for small minds but large knowledge in a small mind is worse than knowing too little too late and ignoring the fact that, though pumpkins are indeed larger, ignorance is bliss'."

"I think I should understand that better," Sun-hee said very politely, "if I had it written down: but I ca'n't quite follow it as you say it."

"That's nothing to what I could say if I choose," Concubine Ok-baem replied, in a pleased tone.

"Pray don't trouble yourself to say it any longer than that," said Sun-hee.

"Oh, don't talk about trouble!" about Ok-baem. "I make you a present of everything I've said as yet."

"A cheap sort of present!" thought Sun-hee. "I'm glad people don't give *Chuseok-presents* like that!" But she did not venture to say it out loud.

"Thinking again?" Concubine Ok-baem asked, with another dig of her hair pin.

"I've a right to think," said Sun-hee sharply, for she was beginning to feel a little worried.

"Just about as much right," said Concubine Ok-baem, "as pigs have to fly; and the m—"

But here, to Sun-hee's great surprise, Concubine Ok-baem's voice died away, even in the middle of her favourite word "moral", and the arm that was linked into hers began to tremble. Sun-hee looked up, and there stood the Queen of *Hwatu* in front of them, with her arms folded, frowning like a thunderstorm.

"A fine day, your Majesty!" Concubine Ok-baem began in a low, weak voice.

"Now, I give you fair warning," shouted the Queen, stamping on the ground as she spoke; "either you or your head must be off, and that in about half no time! Take your choice!"

Concubine Ok-baem took her choice, and was gone in a moment.

The Queen of *Hwatu* said to Sun-hee "Have you seen the Mock Turtleboat yet?"

"No," said Sun-hee. "It seems I've heard mentioned something of a Mock Turtleboat, but I'm not sure what it is."

"Come on, then," said the Queen, "and he shall tell you his history."

They very soon came upon a Phoenix, lying fast asleep in the sun. "Up, lazy thing!" said the Queen, "and take this young lady to see the Mock Turtleboat, and to hear his history. I must go back and see after some executions I have ordered," and she walked off, leaving Sun-hee alone with the Phoenix. Sun-hee did not quite like the look of the creature, but on the whole she thought it would be quite as safe to stay with it as to go after that savage Queen: so she waited.

The Phoenix sat up and rubbed its eyes: then it watched the Queen till she was out of sight: then it chuckled. 'What fun!" said the Phoenix, half to itself, half to Sun-hee.

"What is the fun?" said Sun-hee.

"Why, *she*," said the Phoenix, "it's all her fancy that; they execute never, you know. Come on!"

So they went up to the Mock Turtleboat, who looked at them with large eyes full of tears, but said nothing.

"Young lady this here," said the Phoenix, "your history she does want." "I'll tell it to her," said the Mock Turtleboat in a deep hollow tone. "Sit down, both of you, and don't speak a word till I've finished."

So they sat down, and nobody spoke for some minutes. Sun-hee thought to herself "I don't see how he can ever finish, if he doesn't begin." But she waited patiently.

"Once," said the Mock Turtleboat at last, with a deep sigh, "I was a real Turtleboat."

These words were followed by a very long silence, broken only by an occasional exclamation of "Hjckrrh!" from the Phoenix, and the constant heavy sobbing of the Mock Turtleboat. Sun-hee was very nearly getting up and saying, "Thank you, Sir, for your interesting story," but she could not help thinking there must be more to come, so she sat still and said nothing.

"When I was young and my iron shiny," the Mock Turtleboat went on at last, more calmly, though still sobbing a little now and then, "I was in the company of an armada of Turtleboats and we fought side-by-side in the great tradition of war."

"You mean 'battle', don't you?" Sun-hee asked.

"I say 'tradition' because we always won our battles," said the Mock Turtleboat angrily. "Really you are very dull!"

"Ashamed you should be for telling such a simple question," added the Phoenix; and then they both sat silent and looked at poor Sun-hee, who felt like digging into the sand like a clam. At last the Phoenix said to the Mock Turtleboat "Sail on, old fellow! Don't be all day about it!" and he went on in these words:—

"We were under the command of Admiral Yi—Ah, it was a great victory, though you may not believe it—" "I never said

I didn't," interrupted Sun-hee. "You did," said the Mock Turtleboat.

"Hold your tongue!" added the Phoenix, before Sun-hee could speak again. The Mock Turtleboat went on.

"Before the battle, large pots of *kimchi* were made—hot, red peppers—brought tears to my eyes—"

"Yes," winced Sun-hee "I can imagine."

"They had to do a vesselotomy, you know, and remove my ammunitions," and he began to cry again.

"Oh, that must have been horrid!" said the Phoenix who had also begun to cry.

"Now my hull is empty," the Mock Turtleboat began again, "no more *kimchi* is served, no more battles to win. I'm washed up to shore: my timbers worn, my oars split in half, my aft sunken and sore—"

The Phoenix had begun to wail now, crying "*Aigo, aigo!*" mournfully.

Sun-hee, thinking this had gone on quite far enough, asked, "Do you happen to know any games?"

"Games!" exclaimed the Mock Turtleboat.

"Why of course he does." the Phoenix interrupted in a very decided tone. "Tell her something about the games now."

Chapter X

The Admiral-Quadrille

The Mock Turtleboat sighed deeply, and drew the back of one of the oars across his eyes. He looked at Sun-hee and tried to speak, but, for a moment or two, sobs choked his voice, "Same as if he had a plank in this throat," said the Phoenix; and it set to work shaking him and punching him in the stern. At last the Mock Turtleboat recovered his voice, and with tears running down his cheeks, he went on again:—

"You may not have lived much on the sea—" ("I haven't," said Sun-hee) "—and perhaps you were never even introduced to an armada—" (Sun-hee replied "No, never") "—so you can have no idea what a delightful thing an Admiral-Quadrille is!"

"No, indeed," said Sun-hee, 'What sort of a dance is it?"

"Why," said the Phoenix, "you first form into a line along the sea-shore—"

"Two lines!" cried the Mock Turtleboat. "Junks, galleys, barks, and so on: then, when you've cleared all the anchors out of the way—"

"*That* generally takes some time," interrupted the Phoenix.

"—you advance twice—"

"Each with an Admiral as a partner!" cried the Phoenix.

"Of course," said the Mock Turtleboat scratching one of the planks on his hull. "Advance twice, set to partners—"

"—change Admirals, and come about in same order," continued the Phoenix.

"Then, you know," the Mock Turtleboat went on, "you throw the—"

"The anchors!" shouted the Phoenix, with a bound into the air.

"—as far out to sea as you can—"

"Sail after them!" screamed the Phoenix.

"Turn hard aport in the surf!" cried the Mock Turtleboat, tossing wildly about.

"Change Admirals again!" yelled the Phoenix at the top of its voice.

"Back to land again, run aground, and—that's all the first figure," said the Mock Turtleboat, suddenly dropping his voice; and the two creatures, who had been moving about like mad things all this time, settled down again very sadly and quietly, and looked at Sun-hee.

"It must be a very pretty dance," said Sun-hee timidly.

"Would you like to see a little of it?" said the Mock Turtleboat.

"Very much indeed," said Sun-hee.

"Come, let's try the first figure!" said the Mock Turtleboat to the Phoenix. "We can do it without the Admirals, you know. Which shall we sing?"

"Without the Admirals!" cried the Phoenix. "That would be mutiny!"

"*I'll* sing then," said the Mock Turtleboat. "You've no doubt forgotten the words."

So they began solemnly dancing round and round Sun-hee, every now and then treading on her toes when they passed too close, and waving their oars and wings, respectively, to mark the time, while the Mock Turtleboat sang this, very slowly and sadly:—

"Inside my armoured shell flowed loyalty,
And from my mouth thundered the voice of the military.
Noryang, Noryang, Noryang-o,
The great battle of Noryang Strait.[35]

"Visions of Hansan Island's forested hills,
The blue waters turn red from the glow of the Sun.
Noryang, Noryang, Noryang-o,
The great battle of Noryang Strait.

"As the sun dawns upon the sea,
Yi Sun-shin, strong and calm, held our banner ever still.
Noryang, Noryang, Noryang-o,
The great battle of Noryang Strait.

"Stars there are countless on this night,
Alas, a Great Star falls into the sea.[36]
Noryang, Noryang, Noryang-o,
The great battle of Noryang Strait."[37]

"Thank you, it's a very interesting dance to watch," said Sun-hee, wiping her eyes and feeling very glad it was over at last.

"Shall we try another figure of the Admiral-Quadrille?" asked the Phoenix. "Or would you like the Mock Turtleboat to sing you another song?"

35 Noryang Strait—site of Admiral Yi's last naval battle against the Japanese, in which he was fatally wounded.

36 A Great Star Falls into the Sea—posthumous title appearing on Admiral Yi's shrine in Namhae, overlooking the bay in which he was slain.

37 This poem parodies Korea's most popular folk songs, collectively titled *Ariang,* baving high adaptability for variation, all of which have a deep connection with the emotional life of the people of Korea.

"Oh, a song, please, if the Mock Turtleboat would be so kind," Sun-hee replied, so eagerly that the Phoenix said, in a rather offended tone, "Hm! No accounting for tastes! Sing her '*Kimchi*', will you, old fellow?"

The Mock Turtleboat sighed deeply, and began, in a voice choked with sobs, to sing this:—

"Beautiful Kimchi, so zesty and hot,
Waiting in a Kimchi pot!
Who for such brilliance would not plea?
Kimchi of winter, beautiful Kimchi!
Kimchi of winter, beautiful Kimchi!
Beau—ootiful Kimchi! Beau—ootiful Kimchi!
Kimchii—ii of wi—in—ter,
Beautiful, beautiful Kimchi!

"Beautiful Kimchi! Who cares for eel,
Squid, or any other meal?
Who would not give all else for tu-peag
Won's worth[38] *only of beautiful Kimchi?*
Tu-peag won's worth only of beautiful Kimchi?
Beau—ootiful Kimchi! Beau—ootiful Kimchi!
Kimchii—ii! of wi—in—ter,
Beautiful, beauti—FUL KIMCHI!"

"Chorus again!" cried the Phoenix, and the Mock Turtleboat had just begun to repeat it, when a cry of "The trial's beginning!" was heard in the distance.

"Come on!" cried the Phoenix, and, taking Sun-hee by the hand, it hurried off, without waiting for the end of the song.

"What trial is it?" Sun-hee panted as she ran: but the Phoenix only answered "Come on!" and ran the faster, while

38 *tu-paeg won's worth*—two hundred won (a small sum).

more and more faintly came, carried on the breeze that followed them, the melancholy words:—

> *"Kimchi of wi—in—te—er,*
> *Beautiful, beautiful Kimchi!"*

Chapter XI

Who Stole the Rice Cakes?

The King and Queen of *Hwatu* were seated on their thrones when they arrived, with a great crowd assembled about them—an sorts of little birds and beasts, as well as the whole pack of cards: the Prince was standing before them, in chains, with a soldier on each side to guard him; and near the King was the White Rabbit, with a flute in one hand, and a scroll of rice paper in the other. In the very middle of the court was a table, with a large basket of rice cakes upon it: they looked so good, that it made Sun-hee quite hungry to look at them—"I wish they'd get the trial done," she thought, "and hand round the refreshments!" But there seemed to be no chance of this; so she began looking at everything about her to pass away the time.

Sun-hee had never been to a palace before, but she had heard about them listening to the scholar, and she was quite pleased to find that she knew the name of nearly everything there. "That's the king," she said to herself, "because of his flat, Confucian crown."

"And that's the royal court," thought Sun-hee, Recognizing several of them, she thought, "There's Nam-chul the Dragon, the Pig Baby, the Masked Hare, the Temple-Tiger, a snake from the *yut* game—" then, as she studied them closer, she exclaimed. "Why, they are the twelve creatures of the zodiac!" Then, remembering her own year of birth, concluded that in this curious place, she would have been born in the year of the Pig Baby. "I suppose they are the courtiers." She said this last word two or three times over to herself, being rather proud of it; for she thought, and rightly too, that very few little girls of her age knew the meaning of it at all. However, "courtesans" would have done just as well.

The courtiers were all writing very busily on scrolls. "What are they doing?" Sun-hee whispered to the Phoenix. "They ca'n't have anything to put down yet, before the trial's begun."

"They're putting down their names," the Phoenix whispered in reply, "for fear they should forget them before the end of the trial."

"Stupid things!" Sun-hee began in a loud indignant voice; but she stopped herself hastily, for the White Rabbit cried out "Silence in the court!" and the King peered out from under his large, flat crown to make out who was talking.

Sun-hee could see, as well as if she were looking over their shoulders, that all the courtiers were writing down "Stupid things!" on their scrolls, and she could even make out that one of them didn't know the character for "stupid", and that he had to ask his neighbour to tell him. "A nice mess their scrolls'll be in, before the trial's over!" thought Sun-hee.

One of the courtiers had an ink stone that leaked, and Sun-hee noticed a black stain forming on the hem of her own *hanbok*.[39] This, of course, Sun-hee could not stand, and she

39 *hanbok* (한복)—see note 29 on page 82 above.

went round the court and got behind him, and very soon found the opportunity of replacing the ink with water. She did it so quickly that the poor little creature (it was Nam-chul the Dragon) didn't notice the clear liquid in his black ink stone; so, dipping his brush into the water, he continued to write in this manner the rest of the day; and this was of very little use, as it left no mark on the rice paper.

"Court Musician, read the accusation!" said the King.

On this the White Rabbit blew three modes on the flute, and then unrolled the scroll, and read as follows:—

"The Queen of Hwatu, she made some cakes,
All on a Chuseok Day:
The Prince of Hwatu, he stole those cakes
And took them all away!"

"I have my verdict," the King said to his court.

"Not yet, not yet!" the White Rabbit hastily interrupted. "There's a great deal to come before that!"

"Call the first witness," said the King; and the White Rabbit blew three modes on the flute, and called out "First witness!"

The first witness was the Scholar. He came in with a teacup in one hand and a piece of dried squid in the other. As he kowtowed before the King, a bit of tea spilled from the cup onto the King's robe. The Scholar hastily began rubbing the stain with the squid. "I beg your pardon, your Majesty," be began, "for bringing these in; but I hadn't quite finished my tea when I was sent for."

"You should have finished," said the King, staring hard at the Scholar.

The Scholar looked over and saw entering the Masked Hare, who had followed him into the court, arm-in-arm with the Ginseng.

"Write that down," the King said to the jury; and the jury eagerly wrote down all three dates on their slates, and then added them up, and reduced the answer to *yang* and *bun*.[40]

"And how dare you wear a hat taller than my own!" the King exclaimed, and added, "Remove it at once!"

"I cannot," stated the Scholar.

"*Insolence!*" exclaimed the King, turning to the courtiers, who instantly dipped their brushes in the ink.

"The butterflies will get out," said the Ginseng, and the Scholar looked at him nervously shaking his head.

"Write that down, too," the King said to the courtiers.

"I am a Scholar, your Majesty, and without this particular hat, no one would recognize me," the Scholar added as an explanation. "I'm a Confusion!"

Here the Queen squinted her eyes, and began staring hard at the Scholar, who turned pale and fidgeted. "That, you undoubtedly are—" stated the Queen.

"Give your evidence," said the King; "and don't be nervous, or I'll have you executed on the spot."

This did not seem to encourage the witness at all: he kept giving the King deep bows, and, in his confusion, bit a large piece out of his teacup instead of the dried squid.

Just at this moment Sun-hee felt a very curious sensation, which puzzled her a good deal until she made out what it was: she was beginning to grow larger again, and she thought at first she would get up and leave the palace; but on second thought she decided to remain where she was as long as there was room for her.

"I wish you wouldn't squeeze so," said the Ginseng, who was sitting next to her. "I can hardly breathe."

"I ca'n't help it," said Sun-hee very meekly: "I'm growing."

"You've no right to grow here," said the Ginseng.

40 The *yang* (양/兩) was the currency of Korea between 1892 and 1902. It was subdivided into 10 *jeon* ([MR]*chŏn* 전/錢), 100 *bun* ([MR]*pun* 분/分) and 5 *yang* = 1 *hwan* (환/圜).

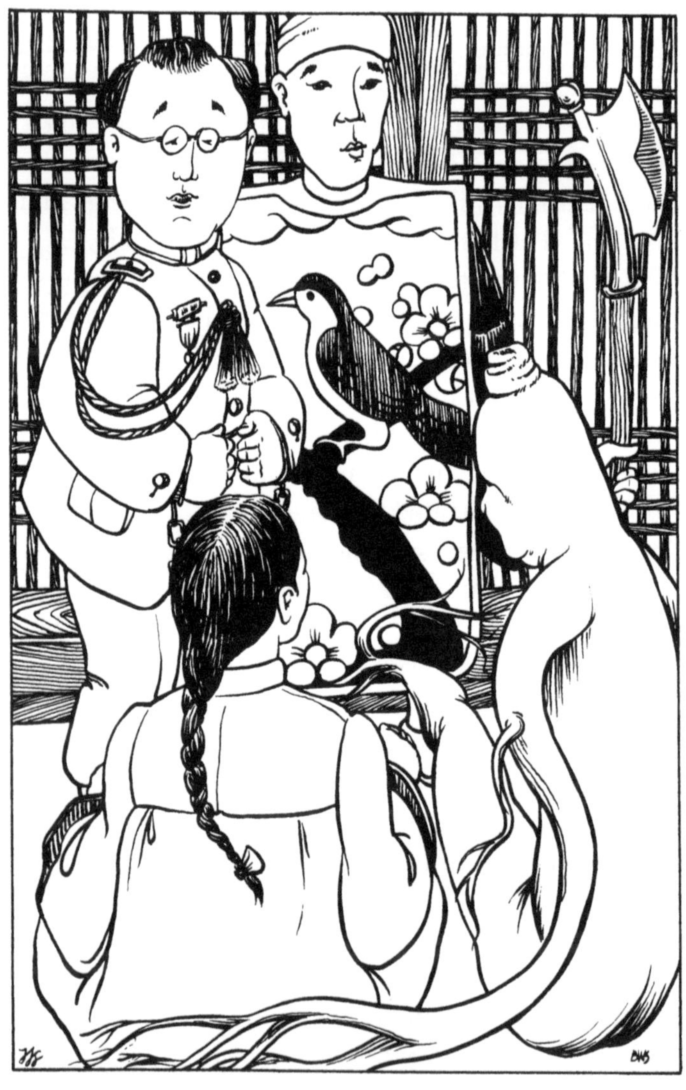

"Don't talk nonsense," said Sun-hee more boldly: "You know you're growing too."

"Yes, but I grow at a very slow pace," said the Ginseng: "not in that ridiculous fashion." And he got up very sulkily and crossed over to the other side of the room.

All this time the Queen had never left off staring at the Scholar, and, just as the Ginseng crossed the court, she said, to the Court Musician, "Bring me the list of the performers in the *Cheoyongmu*!"[41] on which the wretched Scholar trembled so, that on giving another deep bow he banged his forehead against the floor.

"Give your evidence," the King repeated angrily, "or I'll have you executed, whether you are nervous or not."

"I ca'n't remember," said the Scholar.

"You must remember," remarked the King, "or I'll have you executed!"

"'He's as stupid as a borrowed barley-bag'," the Queen whispered to the King.

The miserable Scholar dropped his teacup and dried squid, and kowtowed. "I'm a poor man, your Majesty," he began.

"You're a *very* poor *speaker*," said the King. "If that's all you know about it, you may leave."

"I cannot, your Majesty, as I seem to be stuck in this position," the Scholar said in a muffled voice, still kowtowing.

The Queen left off reading the list of performers to say to one of the soldiers next to the door, "Remove this Scholar's head at once!"

As soon as the Queen had said, "Remove—" the Scholar had jumped up and run outside without even waiting to put his shoes on.

"Call the next witness!" said the King.

The next witness was Concubine Ok-baem's cook. She carried the pepper-pot in her hands, and Sun-hee guessed who

41 *Cheoyongmu* (처용무, MR*Ch'ŏyongmu*)—a traditional court dance.

it was, even before she got into the court, by the way people near the door began wheezing all at once.

"Give your evidence," said the King.

"No," said the cook.

The King looked anxiously at the White Rabbit, who said, in a low voice, "Your Majesty must interrogate *this* witness."

"Well, if I must, I must," the King said with a melancholy air, and after folding his arms and frowning at the cook till his eyes were nearly out of sight, he said, in a deep voice, 'What are *Chuseok* cakes made of?"

"Red pepper, mostly," said the cook.

"Garlic," said a sleepy voice behind her.

"Uproot that Ginseng!" the Queen shrieked out. "Behead that Ginseng! Turn that Ginseng out of the place! Tie his roots! Pinch him! Off with his whiskers!"

For some minutes the whole court was in confusion, getting the Ginseng turned out, and, by the time they had settled down again, the cook had disappeared.

"Never mind!" said the King, with an air of great relief. "Call the next witness." And he added, in an undertone to the Queen, "Really, my dear, you must interrogate the next witness. It quite makes my stomach ache!" He then called out to the White Rabbit who was fumbling over the list of witnesses, "Bring me some seaweed soup for my stomach!"

The White Rabbit sent one of the Queen's maid servants off to find the seaweed soup then glanced down at the list of witnesses. "They haven't got much evidence yet," Sun-hee said to herself, very anxious to see what the next witness would be like. Imagine her surprise, when the White Rabbit read out, at the top of his shrill little voice, the name "Sun-hee!"

CHAPTER XII

Sun-hee's Evidence

"Aigo!" cried Sun-hee, quite forgetting in the flurry of the moment how large she had grown in the last few minutes, and she jumped up in such a hurry that she tipped over several of the courtiers who had been sitting on the edge of her *hanbok*. They lay there sprawling about, reminding her very much of a basket of eels she had accidentally upset the week before.

"Oh, I beg your pardon!" she exclaimed in a tone of great dismay, and began picking them up again as quickly as she could, for the accident of the eels kept running in her head, and she had a vague sort of idea that they must be collected at once and put back into place, or they would be skinned.

As soon as the courtiers had recovered a little from the shock of being upset, and their ink stones filled and brushes found, they set to work very diligently to write out a history of the accident.

"What do you know about this business?" the King said to Sun-hee.

"Nothing," said Sun-hee.

"Nothing *whatever?*" persisted the King.

"Nothing whatever," said Sun-hee.

"That's very important," the King said, turning to the courtiers. They were just beginning to write this down on their scrolls, when the White Rabbit interrupted: "*Un*important, your Majesty means, of course," he said, in a very respectful tone, but frowning and making faces at him as he spoke.

Some of the courtiers wrote it down "important", and some "unimportant". Sun-hee could see this, as she was near enough to look over their scrolls; "but it doesn't matter a bit," she thought to herself.

At this moment the King, who had been for some time busily reading in a book called out "Silence!" and read out from his book, "Rule Forty-two. *All persons higher than Sorak Mountain*[42] *must leave the palace.*"

Everybody looked at Sun-hee.

"I'm not as high as Sorak Mountain," said Sun-hee.

"You are," said the King.

"Nearly twice as high," added the Queen.

"Well, I wo'n't go, at any rate," said Sun-hee; "besides, that's not a regular rule: you invented it just now."

"It's the oldest rule in the book," said the King.

"Then it should be Number One," said Sun-hee.

The King turned pale and shut his book hastily. "I have considered my verdict," he said to his court, in a low trembling voice.

"There's more evidence to come yet, please your Majesty," said the White Rabbit, jumping up in a great hurry: "this scroll has just been found."

"What's in it?" said the Queen.

"I haven't opened it yet," said the White Rabbit; "but it seems to be a letter, written by the prisoner to—to somebody."

42 Sorak Mountain—third highest peak in southern Korea, widely regarded as one of the most scenic areas in the country.

"It must have been that," said the King, "unless it was written to nobody, which isn't usual, you know."

"Who is it directed to?" said one of the courtiers.

"It isn't directed at all," said the White Rabbit: "in fact, there's no seal on the *outside*." He unrolled the scroll as he spoke, and added "It isn't a letter, after all: it's set of verses."

"Are they in the prisoner's own brush work?" asked another of the courtiers.

"No, they're not," said the White Rabbit, "and that's the queerest thing about it." (The court all looked puzzled.)

"He must have imitated somebody else's calligraphy," said the King. (The courtiers all brightened up again.)

"Please, your Majesty," said the Prince, "I didn't write it, and they ca'n't prove that I did: there's no chop mark on the scroll."

"If you didn't sign it," said the King, "that only makes the matter worse. You must have meant some mischief, or else you'd have impressed your chop mark like an honest man."

There was a general clapping of hands at this: it was the first really clever thing the King had said that day.

"That *proves* his guilt, of course," said the Queen: "so off with—"

"It doesn't prove anything of the sort!" said Sun-hee. "Why, you don't even know what they're about!"

"Read them," said the King.

There was dead silence in the court, while the White Rabbit read out these verses:—

"*The moon lies sliced in two,*
Pinched on its rim to form a smile,
On a blue platter rests fluffy peaks,
Raised on bamboo chopsticks into heaven's mouth."[43]

43 This poem roughly parodies a poem traditionally attributed to Kim Sakkat (1807–1863), beginning "Rolled in the hands like rounded hen's eggs…" See *Humor in Korean Literature,* Si-sa-yong-o-sa, Seoul, 1982.

"That's the most important piece of evidence we've heard yet," said the King, rubbing his hands; "so my verdict is—"

"If anyone of them can explain it," said Sun-hee (she had grown so large in the last few minutes that she wasn't a bit afraid of interrupting him), "I'll give him a tael of silver. *I* don't believe there's any meaning in it."

"If there's no meaning in it," said the King, "that saves a world of trouble, you know, as we needn't try to find any. And yet I don't know," he went on, spreading out the verses on his knee, and looking at them with one eye; "I seem to see some meaning' in them, after all. '*—Pinched on its rim—*' you don't go about pinching things do you?" he added, turning to the Prince.

The Prince shook his head sadly. "Do I look like it?" he said (which he certainly did not, as his hands were bound by chains).

"All right, so far," said the king; and he went on muttering over the verses to himself: "'*The moon lies*'—that's this moon-faced Prince, of course—'*sliced in two*'—that must be the Queen and her chopping—'*On a blue platter rests fluffy peaks*' (at that moment there was a disturbance in the back of the court as it appeared that Concubine Ok-baem had knocked over a small screen. "Silence!" the King hissed and then continued)—'*Raised on bamboo chopsticks*' why, that must be what he did with the rice cakes, you know—"

"But it goes on '*into heaven's mouth*'," said Sun-hee.

"Why, there they are!" said the King triumphantly, pointing to the rice cakes on the sacrificial table. "Nothing can be clearer than that. Then again—'*to form a smile*'—you never do smile, my dear, I think?" he said to the Queen.

"Never!" said the Queen, furiously, throwing an ink stone at the Dragon as she spoke. (The unfortunate little Nam-chul had left off writing on his scroll with his water soaked brush, as he found it made no mark; but he now hastily began again, using the ink, that was trickling down his face, as long as it lasted.)

"'No one strikes a smiling face," said the King looking round the court with a smile. There was a dead silence.

"It's a proverb!" the King added in an angry tone, and everyone smiled. "Let me give my verdict," the King said, for about the twentieth time that day.

"No, no!" said the Queen. "Flogging first—verdict afterwards."

"'The ant shakes a beech tree!'" said Sun-hee loudly.

"Hold your tongue!" said the Queen, turning purple.

"I wo'n't!" said Sun-hee.

"Off with her head!" the Queen shouted at he top of her voice. Nobody moved.

"Who cares for you?" said Sun-hee (she had grown to her full size by this time). "You're nothing but a pack of cards!"

At this moment the whole pack rose up into the air, and came flying down upon her; she gave a little scream, half of fright and half of anger, and tried to beat them off, and found herself lying under the gingko tree, with her head in the lap of her sister, who was gently brushing away some dead leaves that had fluttered down from the trees upon her face.

"Wake up, Sun-hee dear!" said her sister. "Why, what a long sleep you've had!"

"Oh, I've had such a curious dream!" said Sun-hee. And she told her sister, as well as she could remember them, all these strange Adventures of hers that you have just been reading about; and, when she had finished, her sister kissed her, and said "It was a curious dream, dear, certainly; but now hurry and brush yourself off: it's getting late," So Sun-hee brushed the grass from her *hanbok* and started off to find her Mother, thinking while she ran, as well she might, what a wonderful dream it had been.

But her sister sat still just as she left her, leaning her head on her hand, watching the setting sun, and thinking of little Sun-hee and all her wonderful Adventures, till she too began dreaming after a fashion, and this was her dream:—

First, she dreamed about little Sun-hee herself: once again the tiny hands were clasped upon her knee, and the bright eager eyes were looking up into hers—she could hear the very tones of her voice, and see that queer little toss of her head to keep back the wandering hair that would always get into her eyes—and still as she listened or seemed to listen, the whole place around her became alive with the strange creatures of her little sister's dream.

The long grass rustled at her feet as the White Rabbit hurried by, his white *jeogori* flapping in the wind—she could hear the rattle of the teacups as the Masked Hare poured tea for the Scholar; the Ginseng pulling up his roots and walking around—she could hear the shrill voice of the Queen of *Hwatu* ordering off her unfortunate guests to execution—once more the Pig Baby was wheezing on Concubine Ok-baem's knee, while bowls and kettles crashed around it—once more the shriek of the Phoenix, the splashing of water from the Dragon's ink stone, and the clanking of chains tied around the unfortunate Prince, filled the air, mixed up with the distant sobs of the miserable Mock Turtleboat.

So she sat on with closed eyes, and half believed herself Under the Land of Morning Calm, though she knew she had but to open them again, and all would change in dull reality—the grass would be only rustled by the breeze, and the leaves flapping on gusts of wind—the rattling teacups would change to the sounds of a farmer's dance in the schoolyard; and the Ginseng's meanderings to the sounds of a ground squirrel gathering the fallen gingko nuts—the Queen's shrill cries to the calls of a magpie—and the wheeze of the baby, the shriek of the Phoenix, and an the other queer noises, would change (she knew) to the confused clamour of the busy village—while the lowing of the cattle in the distance would take the place of the Mock Turtleboat's heavy sobs.

Lastly, she pictured to herself how this same little sister of hers would, in the after-time, be herself a grown woman: and how she would keep, through all her riper years, the simple and loving heart of her childhood: and how she would gather about her other little children, and make *their* eyes bright and eager with many a strange tale, perhaps even with the dream Under the Land of Morning Calm of long ago and how she would feel with all their simple sorrows, and find pleasure in all their simple joys, remembering her own child-life, and the happy *Chuseok* days.

SOURCES

Alice's Adventures in Wonderland: The Evertype definitive edition, by Lewis Carroll, 2016

Alice's Adventures in Wonderland, illus. June Lornie, 2013

Alice's Adventures in Wonderland, illus. Mathew Staunton, 2015

Alice's Adventures in Wonderland, illus. Harry Furniss, 2016

Through the Looking-Glass and What Alice Found There, by Lewis Carroll 2009

The Nursery "Alice", by Lewis Carroll, 2015

Alice's Adventures under Ground, by Lewis Carroll, 2009

The Hunting of the Snark, by Lewis Carroll, 2010

SEQUELS

A New Alice in the Old Wonderland, by Anna Matlack Richards, 2009

New Adventures of Alice, by John Rae, 2010

Alice Through the Needle's Eye, by Gilbert Adair, 2012

Wonderland Revisited and the Games Alice Played There, by Keith Sheppard, 2009

Alice and the Boy who Slew the Jabberwock, by Allan William Parkes, 2016

SPELLING

Alice's Adventures in Wonderland, Retold in words of one Syllable by Mrs J. C. Gorham, 2010

𐐈𐑊𐐮𐑅'𐑆 𐐈𐐼𐑂𐐯𐑌𐐽𐐲𐑉𐑆 𐐮𐑌 𐐎𐐲𐑌𐐼𐐲𐑉𐑊𐐰𐑌𐐼, *Alice* printed in the Deseret Alphabet, 2014

𐐜 𐐐𐐲𐑌𐐻𐐮𐑍 𐐲𐑂 𐑄 𐐝𐑌𐐫𐑉𐐿, *The Hunting of the Snark* printed in the Deseret Alphabet, 2016

𐐛𐑉𐐭 𐑄 𐐢𐐳𐐿𐐮𐑍-𐐘𐑊𐐰𐑅 𐐰𐑌𐐼 𐐐𐐶𐐲𐐻 𐐈𐑊𐐮𐑅 𐐙𐐵𐑌𐐼 𐐜𐐯𐑉, *Looking-Glass* printed in the Deseret Alphabet, 2016

Alice's Adventures in Wonderland,
Alice printed in Dyslexic-Friendly fonts, 2015

[illegible],
Alice printed in a font that simulates Dyslexia, 2015

[illegible],
Alice printed in the Ewellic Alphabet, 2013

'Ælɪsɪz əd'ventʃəz ɪn 'Wʌndəˌlænd,
Alice printed in the International Phonetic Alphabet, 2014

Alis'z Advnčrz in Wunḍland, *Alice* printed in the Ñspel orthography, 2015

[illegible],
Alice printed in the Nyctographic Square Alphabet, 2011

[illegible], *Alice* printed in the Shaw Alphabet, 2013

ALISIZ ADVENCƎRZ IN WUNDЯLAND,
Alice printed in the Unifon Alphabet, 2014

[illegible] (Aliz kalandjai Csodaországban),
The Hungarian *Alice* printed in Old Hungarian script, tr. Anikó Szilágyi, 2016

SCHOLARSHIP

Reflecting on Alice: A Textual Commentary on *Through the Looking-Glass*, by Selwyn Goodacre, 2016

Elucidating Alice: A Textual Commentary on *Alice's Adventures in Wonderland*, by Selwyn Goodacre, 2015

Behind the Looking-Glass: Reflections on the Myth of Lewis Carroll, by Sherry L. Ackerman, 2012

Selections from the Lewis Carroll Collection of Victoria J. Sewell, compiled by Byron W. Sewell, 2014

SOCIAL COMMENTARY

Clara in Blunderland, by Caroline Lewis, 2010

Lost in Blunderland: The further adventures of Clara, by Caroline Lewis, 2010

John Bull's Adventures in the Fiscal Wonderland, by Charles Geake, 2010

Also available from Evertype

The Westminster Alice, by H. H. Munro (Saki), 2010

Alice in Blunderland: An Iridescent Dream,
by John Kendrick Bangs, 2010

Simulations

Davy and the Goblin, by Charles Edward Carryl, 2010

The Admiral's Caravan, by Charles Edward Carryl, 2010

Gladys in Grammarland, by Audrey Mayhew Allen, 2010

Alice's Adventures in Pictureland, by Florence Adèle Evans, 2011

Folly in Fairyland, by Carolyn Wells, 2016

Rollo in Emblemland, by J. K. Bangs & C. R. Macauley, 2010

Phyllis in Piskie-land, by J. Henry Harris, 2012

Alice in Beeland, by Lillian Elizabeth Roy, 2012

Eileen's Adventures in Wordland, by Zillah K. Macdonald, 2010

Alice and the Time Machine, by Victor Fet, 2016

Алиса и Машина Времени (Alisa i Mashina Vremeni),
Alice and the Time Machine in Russian, tr. Victor Fet, 2016

Sewelliana

Sun-hee's Adventures Under the Land of Morning Calm,
by Victoria J. Sewell & Byron W. Sewell, 2016

선희의 조용한 아침의 나라 모험기
(Seonhuiui Joyonghan Achim-ui Nala Moheomgi),
Sun-hee in Korean, tr. Miyeong Kang, 2016

Alix's Adventures in Wonderland:
Lewis Carroll's Nightmare, by Byron W. Sewell, 2011

Áloþk's Adventures in Goatland, by Byron W. Sewell, 2011

Alice's Bad Hair Day in Wonderland, by Byron W. Sewell, 2012

The Carrollian Tales of Inspector Spectre, by Byron W. Sewell, 2011

The Annotated Alice in Nurseryland, by Byron W. Sewell, 2016

The Haunting of the Snarkasbord, by Alison Tannenbaum, Byron W. Sewell, Charlie Lovett, & August A. Imholtz, Jr, 2012

Snarkmaster, by Byron W. Sewell, 2012

In the Boojum Forest, by Byron W. Sewell, 2014

Murder by Boojum, by Byron W. Sewell, 2014

Close Encounters of the Snarkian Kind, by Byron W. Sewell, 2016

TRANSLATIONS

Кайкалдыҥ Јеринде Алисала болгон учуралдар (Kaykaldıñ Cerinde Alisala bolgon uçuraldar), *Alice* in Altai, tr. Küler Tepukov, 2016

Alice's Adventures in An Appalachian Wonderland, *Alice* in Appalachian English, tr. Byron & Victoria Sewell, 2012

Patimatli ali Alice tu Văsilia ti Ciudii, *Alice* in Aromanian, tr. Mariana Bara, 2015

Алесіны прыгоды ў Цудазем'і (Alesiny pryhody u Tsudazem'i), *Alice* in Belarusian, tr. Max Ščur, 2016

На тым баку Люстра і што там напаткала Алесю (Na tym baku Liustra i shto tam napatkala Alesiu), *Looking-Glass* in Belarusian, tr. Max Ščur, 2016

Снаркаловы (Snarkalovy), *The Hunting of the Snark* in Belarusian, tr. Max Ščur, 2016

Crystal's Adventures in A Cockney Wonderland, *Alice* in Cockney Rhyming Slang, tr. Charlie Lovett, 2015

Aventurs Alys in Pow an Anethow, *Alice* in Cornish, tr. Nicholas Williams, 2015

Alice's Ventures in Wunderland, *Alice* in Cornu-English, tr. Alan M. Kent, 2015

Alices Hændelser i Vidunderlandet, *Alice* in Danish, tr. D.G., Forthcoming

آلیس در سرزمین عجایب (Âlis dar Sarzamin-e Ajâyeb),
Alice in Dari, tr. Rahman Arman, 2015

La Aventuroj de Alicio en Mirlando,
Alice in Esperanto, tr. E. L. Kearney (1910), 2009

La Aventuroj de Alico en Mirlando,
Alice in Esperanto, tr. Donald Broadribb, 2012

Trans la Spegulo kaj kion Alico trovis tie,
Looking-Glass in Esperanto, tr. Donald Broadribb, 2012

Les Aventures d'Alice au pays des merveilles,
Alice in French, tr. Henri Bué, 2015

Les Aventures d'Alice au pays des merveilles,
Alice in French, tr. Henri Bué, illus. Mathew Staunton, 2015

Alisanın Gezisi Şaşilacek Yerdä,
Alice in Gagauz, tr. Ilya Karaseni, 2016

ელისის თავგადასავალი საოცრებათა ქვეყანაში
(Elisis t'avgadasavali saoc'rebat'a k'veqanaši),
Alice in Georgian, tr. Giorgi Gokieli, 2016

Alice's Abenteuer im Wunderland,
Alice in German, tr. Antonie Zimmermann, 2010

Die Lissel ehr Erlebnisse im Wunnerland,
Alice in Palantine German, tr. Franz Schlosser, 2013

Der Alice ihre Obmteier im Wunderlaund,
Alice in Viennese German, tr. Hans Werner Sokop, 2012

Balþos Gadedeis Aþalhaidais in Sildaleikalanda,
Alice in Gothic, tr. David Alexander Carlton, 2015

Nā Hana Kupanaha a ʻĀleka ma ka ʻĀina Kamahaʻo,
Alice in Hawaiian, tr. R. Keao NeSmith, 2016

Ma Loko o ke Aniani Kū a me ka Mea i Loaʻa iā ʻĀleka ma Laila, *Looking-Glass* in Hawaiian, tr. R. Keao NeSmith, 2016

Aliz kalandjai Csodaországban,
Alice in Hungarian, tr. Anikó Szilágyi, 2013

Eachtra Eibhlíse i dTír na nIontas,
Alice in Irish, tr. Pádraig Ó Cadhla (1922), 2015

Eachtraí Eilíse i dTír na nIontas, *Alice* in Irish, tr. Nicholas Williams, 2007

Lastall den Scáthán agus a bhFuair Eilís Ann Roimpi,
Looking-Glass in Irish, tr. Nicholas Williams, 2009

Le Avventure di Alice nel Paese delle Meraviglie,
Alice in Italian, tr. Teodorico Pietrocòla Rossetti, 2010

Alis Advencha ina Wandalan,
Alice in Jamaican Creole, tr. Tamirand Nnena De Lisser, 2016

L's Aventuthes d'Alice en Êmèrvil'lie,
Alice in Jèrriais, tr. Geraint Williams, 2012

L'Travèrs du Mitheux et chein qu'Alice y dêmuchit,
Looking-Glass in Jèrriais, tr. Geraint Williams, 2012

Әлисәнің ғажайып елдегі басынан кешкендері
(Älïsäniñ ğajayıp eldegi basınan keşkenderi),
Alice in Kazakh, tr. Fatima Moldashova, 2016

Алисанын Кызыктар Өлкөсүндөгү укмуштуу окуялары
(Alisanın Kızıktar Ölkösündögü ukmuştuu okuyaları),
Alice in Kyrgyz, tr. Aida Egemberdieva, 2016

Las Aventuras de Alisia en el Paiz de las Maraviyas,
Alice in Ladino, tr. Avner Perez, 2016

לאס אב'ינטוראס די אליסייה אין איל פאאיס די לאס מאראב'ילייאס
(Las Aventuras de Alisia en el Paiz de las Maraviyas),
Alice in Ladino, tr. Avner Perez, 2016

Alisis pīdzeivuojumi Breinumu zemē,
Alice in Latgalian, tr. Evika Muizniece, 2015

Alicia in Terra Mirabili, *Alice* in Latin, tr. Clive Harcourt Carruthers, 2011

Aliciae per Speculum Trānsitus (Quaeque Ibi Invēnit),
Looking-Glass in Latin, tr. Clive Harcourt Carruthers, Forthcoming

Alisa-ney Aventuras in Divalanda, *Alice* in Lingua de Planeta (Lidepla), tr.
Anastasia Lysenko & Dmitry Ivanov, 2014

La aventuras de Alisia en la pais de mervelias,
Alice in Lingua Franca Nova, tr. Simon Davies, 2012

Alice ẹhr Ẹventüürn in't Wunnerland,
Alice in Low German, tr. Reinhard F. Hahn, 2010

Contoyrtyssyn Ealish ayns Çheer ny Yindyssyn,
Alice in Manx, tr. Brian Stowell, 2010

Ko Ngā Takahanga i a Ārihi i Te Ao Mīharo,
Alice in Māori, tr. Tom Roa, 2015

Dee Erläwnisse von Alice em Wundalaund,
Alice in Mennonite Low German, tr. Jack Thiessen, 2012

Auanturiou adelis en Bro an Marthou,
Alice in Middle Breton, tr. Herve Le Bihan & Herve Kerrain, Forthcoming

The Aventures of Alys in Wondyr Lond,
Alice in Middle English, tr. Brian S. Lee, 2013

L'Avventure d'Alice 'int' 'o Paese d' 'e Maraveglie,
Alice in Neapolitan, tr. Roberto D'Ajello, 2016

L'Aventuros de Alis in Marvoland, *Alice* in Neo, tr. Ralph Midgley, 2013

Elises Eventyr i Undernes Land: den første norske *Alice*:
Elise's Adventures in the Land of Wonders: the first Norwegian *Alice*,
Alice in Norwegian, ed. & tr. Anne Kristin Lande, 2016

Æðelgȳðe Ellendǽda on Wundorlande,
Alice in Old English, tr. Peter S. Baker, 2015

La geste d'Aalis el Païs de Merveilles,
Alice in Old French, tr. May Plouzeau, 2016

Alitjilu Palyantja Tjuta Ngura Tjukurmankuntjala (Alitji's Adventures in Dreamland), *Alice* in Pitjantjatjara, tr. Nancy Sheppard, 2016

Alitji's Adventures in Dreamland: An Aboriginal tale inspired by *Alice's Adventures in Wonderland*, adapted by Nancy Sheppard, 2016

Alice Contada aos Mais Pequenos,
The Nursery "Alice" in Portuguese, tr., Rogério Miguel Puga, 2015

Соня въ царствѣ дива (Sonia v tsarstvie diva):
Sonja in a Kingdom of Wonder,
Alice in facsimile of the 1879 first Russian translation, 2013

Охота на Снарка (Okhota na Snarka),
The Hunting of the Snark in Russian, tr. Victor Fet, 2016

Ia Aventures as Alice in Daumsenland,
Alice in Sambahsa, tr. Olivier Simon, 2013

Ocolo id Specule ed Quo Alice Trohv Ter,
Looking-Glass in Sambahsa, tr. Olivier Simon, 2016

ʻO Tāfaoga a ʻĀlise i le Nuʻu o Mea Ofoofogia,
Alice in Samoan, tr. Luafata Simanu-Klutz, 2013

Eachdraidh Ealasaid ann an Tìr nan Iongantas,
Alice in Scottish Gaelic, tr. Moray Watson, 2012

Alice's Adventchers in Wunderland,
Alice in Scouse, tr. Marvin R. Sumner, 2015

Mbalango wa Alice eTikweni ra Swihlamariso,
Alice in Shangani, tr. Peniah Mabaso & Steyn Khesani Madlome, 2015

Ahlice's Aveenturs in Wunderlaant,
Alice in Border Scots, tr. Cameron Halfpenny 2015

Alice's Mishanters in e Land o Farlies,
Alice in Caithness Scots, tr. Catherine Byrne 2014

Alice's Adventirs in Wunnerlaun,
Alice in Glaswegian Scots, tr. Thomas Clark, 2014

Ailice's Anters in Ferlielann,
Alice in North-East Scots (Doric), tr. Derrick McClure, 2012

Alice's Adventirs in Wonderlaand,
Alice in Shetland Scots, tr. Laureen Johnson, 2012

Ailice's Àventurs in Wunnerland,
Alice in Southeast Central Scots, tr. Sandy Fleemin, 2011

Ailis's Anterins i the Laun o Ferlies,
Alice in Synthetic Scots, tr. Andrew McCallum, 2013

Alice's Carrànts in Wunnerlan,
Alice in Ulster Scots, tr. Anne Morrison-Smyth, 2013

Alison's Jants in Ferlieland,
Alice in West-Central Scots, tr. James Andrew Begg, 2014

Alice muNyika yeMashiripiti,
Alice in Shona, tr. Shumirai Nyota & Tsitsi Nyoni, 2015

Алисаның қайғаллығ Черинде полған чоруқтары
(Alisanyñ qayğallyğ Çerinde polğan çoruqtarı),
Alice in Shor, tr. Liubov′ Arbachakova, 2016

Alis bu Cëlmo dac Cojube w dat Tantelat,
Alice in Ṣurayt, tr. Jan Beṭ-Ṣawoce, 2015

Alisi Ndani ya Nchi ya Ajabu, *Alice* in Swahili, tr. Ida Hadjuvayanis, 2015

Alices Äventyr i Sagolandet, *Alice* in Swedish, tr. Emily Nonnen, 2010

'Alisi 'i he Fonua 'o e Fakaofo',
Alice in Tongan, tr. Siutāula Cocker & Telesia Kalavite, 2014

Ventürs jiela Lälid in Stunalän, *Alice* in Volapük, tr. Ralph Midgley, 2016

Lès-avirètes da Alice ô payis dès mèrvèyes,
Alice in Walloon, tr. Jean-Luc Fauconnier, 2012

Anturiaethau Alys yng Ngwlad Hud, *Alice* in Welsh, tr. Selyf Roberts, 2010

I Avventur de Alìs ind el Paes di Meravili,
Alice in Western Lombard, tr. GianPietro Gallinelli, 2015

Di Avantures fun Alis in Vunderland,
Alice in Yiddish, tr. Joan Braman, 2015

Alises Avantures in Vunderland,
Alice in Yiddish, tr. Adina Bar-El, Forthcoming

Insumansumane Zika-Alice,
Alice in Zimbabwean Ndebele, tr. Dion Nkomo, 2015

U-Alice Ezweni Lezimanga, *Alice* in Zulu, tr. Bhekinkosi Ntuli, 2014

www.ingramcontent.com/pod-product-compliance
Ingram Content Group UK Ltd.
Pitfield, Milton Keynes, MK11 3LW, UK
UKHW041823200726
13854UKWH00002BA/513